Lucie crept

She slipped one hand inside the ~~~~~~~ four-poster. She thought she could hear him breathing. Her palm closed on warm, smooth skin. Oh yeah, he was in there.

The bed frame squeaked as she moved across the mattress. Her fingers slid over the firm ridges of his ribs, the strong expanse of his muscled torso.

"Is that you?" she whispered, even as she knew that no way in hell that chest belonged to safe, reliable Baker Burns.

What was worse, she didn't care!

His hand snagged her wrist suddenly, hauling her on top of him. She was sliding up his body, taking in the hard feel of him against her skin. A moan of pure bliss escaped her lips. He groaned almost in unison.

Had she ever felt pleasure like this? Not a chance!

She pressed closer, fitting herself to his long, lean body, making herself tingle from head to toe. So this was what a fling felt like. Like one big beautifully wrapped package that she got to keep opening all night long.

Lucie smiled wickedly into the darkness. *Oh, yeah. Happy birthday to me....*

Dear Reader,

Some of my favorite authors and dearest friends have
written for Harlequin Temptation over the years, so
I was absolutely delighted to get the chance to write
Just a Little Fling for this terrific line. I love fast-paced,
sexy, funny books, so THE WRONG BED miniseries
seemed like the perfect place for me under the
Harlequin Temptation umbrella.

As I mused on the Wrong Bed theme, I came up
with all kinds of intriguing ideas. After all, I thought,
what could be more fun than a hotel full of gorgeous
groomsmen, all wearing kilts at a Scottish-themed
nightmare of a wedding, too many similar keys,
identical bridesmaids' bags and one plucky bridesmaid
facing her thirtieth birthday in desperate need of a
little fling? It worked for me. I had a wonderful time
writing the story, and I hope you enjoy it, too!

Cheers!

Julie Kistler

Books by Julie Kistler

HARLEQUIN DUETS
19—CALLING MR. RIGHT
30—IN BED WITH THE WILD ONE

HARLEQUIN AMERICAN ROMANCE
740—TUESDAY'S KNIGHT
782—LIZZIE'S LAST-CHANCE FIANCÉ

Don't miss any of our special offers. Write to us at the
following address for information on our newest releases.

Harlequin Reader Service
U.S.: 3010 Walden Ave., P.O. Box 1325, Buffalo, NY 14269
Canadian: P.O. Box 609, Fort Erie, Ont. L2A 5X3

JUST A LITTLE FLING
Julie Kistler

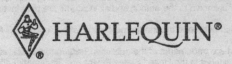

HARLEQUIN®

TORONTO • NEW YORK • LONDON
AMSTERDAM • PARIS • SYDNEY • HAMBURG
STOCKHOLM • ATHENS • TOKYO • MILAN • MADRID
PRAGUE • WARSAW • BUDAPEST • AUCKLAND

To Vicki Lewis Thompson, Temptation doyenne, and to Birgit, who is such a pleasure to work with

ISBN 0-373-25908-5

JUST A LITTLE FLING

Copyright © 2000 by Julie Kistler.

All rights reserved. Except for use in any review, the reproduction or utilization of this work in whole or in part in any form by any electronic, mechanical or other means, now known or hereafter invented, including xerography, photocopying and recording, or in any information storage or retrieval system, is forbidden without the written permission of the publisher, Harlequin Enterprises Limited, 225 Duncan Mill Road, Don Mills, Ontario, Canada M3B 3K9.

All characters in this book have no existence outside the imagination of the author and have no relation whatsoever to anyone bearing the same name or names. They are not even distantly inspired by any individual known or unknown to the author, and all incidents are pure invention.

This edition published by arrangement with Harlequin Books S.A.

® and TM are trademarks of the publisher. Trademarks indicated with ® are registered in the United States Patent and Trademark Office, the Canadian Trade Marks Office and in other countries.

Visit us at www.eHarlequin.com

Printed in U.S.A.

1

LUCIE WEBSTER WAS already itching to bolt the chapel—and they weren't even up to "Do you take this man?"

Lucky thing it wasn't her wedding, or she would've.

But no, it was her much younger half sister, Steffi, who was tying the knot. With nine years between them, she and Steffi had never been close, which put Lucie well down the line at number thirteen in a collection of fifteen bridesmaids. She knew she was picked out of desperation—it was hard to come up with fifteen willing attendants, for goodness sake—but she could hardly say no when her father started twisting arms on behalf of his beloved Steffi.

So here she was, squashed together with the other losers at the end of the line, right where they ran out of space around the altar and had to sort of huddle against a stone wall. Well, she thought, trying to look on the bright side, at least this way she had something to lean on, which took some of the pressure off the nasty, high-heeled granny boots Steffi had chosen for the bridesmaids.

Quietly shifting her weight, Lucie glanced around the chapel. Actually, this place was rather pretty, in a gloomy, Gothic way, with crumbling stone and flickering candles giving it a romantic glow.

It did seem kind of strange as churches went. But what could you expect from a chapel attached to a golf course? If someone needed divine intervention to get out of a sand trap, this would be the place to turn. Still, Lucie felt sure it wasn't intended for a crowded, over-perfumed spectacle like this one. Under the circumstances, St. Andrew's Chapel felt more like Sardines R Us.

Plus, Steffi's super-Scottish theme had necessitated itchy kilts and even itchier wool jackets for the whole bridal party. Except for Steffi herself, of course. She was radiant in a white lace dress that stood out like a beacon in this sea of dark, rather menacing, red-and-black tartans.

Maybe it was the overabundance of plaid making Lucie swoon. That or the heat of a sultry June evening, the close conditions, the thick odor of roses and melting wax, or the tight, uncomfortable clothing.

As the voices up in front droned on, Lucie used her bouquet as a block so she could reach inside her kilt and give her waistline a good scratch.

"Aaah," she breathed. More dirty looks. Well, good grief, it wasn't her fault if Steffi'd stuck them all in these silly outfits. So she was marrying a guy named Mackintosh. So his family owned golf courses and resorts with goofy Scottish names—all "Bonnie Brae" and "Glen Loch Laddie"—all over Chicagoland. Did that mean Steffi had to dredge up kilts and tams and bagpipers out the wazoo just to marry the guy?

Apparently.

Lucie's nose began to tickle. Uh-oh. Sneeze coming on. She tried her best to stifle it into her bouquet, but that made her inhale half a rose petal, and the sneeze came barreling out with a loud "ha-ha-ha-chooooo!"

Oops. A rustle ran up and down the wedding party, and she felt her cheeks flush with warmth.

Par for the course, Steffi stamped her tiny foot, smacked the maid of honor with her bouquet, and demanded, "What was that? Who did that?" Nobody answered her, but they were all craning their necks. Even the best man turned back to see who'd made the rude noise.

The very, very cute best man. Lucie managed a weak smile.

His name was Ian. Even though they hadn't been introduced, she still knew that much. He was the groom's brother, practically a twin, and every single one of the fifteen bridesmaids had had her eye on him since the festivities began. He also looked a heck of a lot better in a skirt than she did.

He caught her eye, sending her a wink—bless his gorgeous heart—and then he turned back to the waning moments of the ceremony like everyone else.

Nice legs. Lucie's smile widened behind her bouquet. What a picker-upper to have someone like Ian Mackintosh wink at her. But, for now, she'd just have to content herself with the view and speculating on what he might be wearing underneath that thing.

"Absolutely nothing," she whispered, feeling a little tingle run down her spine at the very thought.

Guys like Ian—all dark good looks and arrogance sculpted into a dynamite package—would rather die than wear briefs *or* boxers under there. That seemed like a given. But she'd love to check it out, just to be sure. What would the petulant bride do if her half sister dropped to her knees and crawled up to the altar to peek under the best man's kilt?

But she didn't. No, she was good. She stood where she was, and she didn't sneeze or scratch or faint or peek or any of the other things she wanted to do.

Finally, blessedly, they got to the end of the ceremony, and the bagpipes geared up for a recessional that rattled the rooftop in the tiny chapel. Steffi and Kyle, the bride and groom, swept down the aisle, with Steffi looking triumphant and Kyle every bit as cute as his brother. Trying not to feel envious of her half sister, Lucie waited her turn to make tracks as well. As she hung back in position number thirteen, she found herself singing something under her breath, but it wasn't remotely what the pipers were playing.

No, it was "Happy Birthday."

"Happy birthday to me," she hummed defiantly, linking up with Baker Burns, her counterpart groomsman, to shuffle slowly out of the chapel. She'd known Baker forever, but not even he had remembered that today was her birthday. Lucie lifted her chin and kept on humming. You only hit the big 3-0 once, after all. Steffi's wedding certainly wasn't her first choice for a proper celebration, but Lucie would make do.

"Having a good time?" Baker asked, pitching his

voice loud enough to be heard over the bagpipes. "Are you singing something?"

He really was a nice man. Except for a thinning hairline, he was exactly the same sweet boy who'd offered her his seat on the bus on the way to seventh grade.

But she didn't want to confide today's humiliating facts, not even to Baker. She'd just keep it to herself that she was turning thirty in about two hours and not one solitary soul had remembered.

"It's nothing," she told him. "Just glad to be out of that church. Phew."

Not that it was any better outside in the still, humid air. Perspiration trickled inside her stiff white blouse, making her feel damp and sticky. She'd done her best to smooth her thick, wavy red hair into a neat bun, as per Steffi's instructions, but she knew little wisps were curling around her hairline and tendrils had escaped at the nape of her neck. In short, she was a mess.

"So where do we go from here?" she asked Baker. "Please tell me it's someplace with really potent air-conditioning."

He lifted an eyebrow. "Don't tell me you weren't listening when Ginetta gave out the orders?"

"Sort of." Actually, she'd tuned out most of it. But she did remember that Steffi and her mother, the hard-as-nails Ginetta, seemed to have this whole wedding party choreographed to within an inch of its life.

"Do not pass Go," Baker continued, mocking Ginetta's snobby, nasal voice. "Do not collect two hundred dollars. Just proceed straight over to the Inn."

"Oh, right." It was all coming back to her now. No

dawdling, no receiving line. Just hurry over to the reception, sit down, be quiet, and await further instructions.

As the wedding procession navigated a short path
from the chapel to the main building, a castle-like
structure called the Highland Inn, Lucie held onto
Baker's arm. The worn pavement was uneven, and the
last thing she wanted to do was topple over and embarrass herself even more.

Looking up as they turned the corner, she caught her
breath. It had rained earlier in the day, creating a soft
mist around the Inn's stone turrets and balconies, making it look as if it had been plucked from the Scottish
highlands and set down intact in the Chicago suburbs.

"It's lovely," she whispered.

"Would it dare be anything else?" Baker asked
wryly.

The Highland Inn was the finest golf resort in the
senior Mr. Mackintosh's empire, and so the natural,
rent-free choice for Steffi's wedding. Lucky Steffi. Except she should've left it as is, instead of adding all the
over-the-top Scottish nonsense. As they ducked inside,
they were hit in the face with cascading plaid fabric,
tons more candles, and bowers of red and black roses
arranged in rows to look as if they were—you guessed
it—plaid. And, of course, the ever-present pipers
wailed away.

As everyone filed in, kilt-clad waiters guided them
to their assigned seats. "Them, too?" Lucie whispered.
"Is there anyone here *not* in a kilt?"

Lucie thought of herself as a free spirit, but this was

too much, even for her. All they needed was the Loch Ness monster rising up from the punch bowl, and the evening would be complete.

"You'd think somebody would've stopped Steffi from going so nuts with this stuff." Grimly, Baker adjusted his own tartan, but his knobby knees were still visible. Poor Baker didn't have the legs for it.

Meanwhile, the ballroom was a beehive of activity, with wedding guests trying to squeeze around the clustered tables to find their wee plaid place cards.

Lucie was much too tired to look at the tiny cards on every single table. So she commandeered a rather surly young man who informed her that he was not a waiter, just a busboy, and as such, was not responsible for figuring out where they were supposed to sit. She should've known he wasn't anyone important—no kilt. But then Baker slipped him a ten, and the bad-tempered busboy managed to scare up a list, after which he led them to a table near the back of the room, where some of the other unpopular members of the wedding party were already parked.

A very lively girl named Delilah, aka bridesmaid number twelve, was pouring champagne. "This has to be the dullest wedding I've ever seen," she complained.

But then she grinned, quickly shedding her red wool jacket and undoing the first few buttons on her shirt. Wiggling, Delilah made a point of showing off some cleavage, which seemed to perk up the cranky busboy hanging over her.

"Hon, can you run get us a couple more bottles of

bubbly?" she inquired. "We're just parched here." As he skedaddled, Delilah raised her glass and called out, "Let's get this party started, shall we?"

Lucie wished she were as brave as Delilah, so cheerfully stripping out of her bridesmaid duds and throwing caution to the winds. *She* was afraid her father or her half sister would come trolling around and yell at her. Still, she did manage to discard her jacket and undo the top button on her blouse, and then fanned herself with the plaid-covered wedding program on the table. Still melting. She definitely needed a drink, and the champagne was handy. It was cold and it was wet, and that was good enough.

But as she tipped up her glass, she caught sight of the best man, the adorable Ian, angling her way, and she almost choked in midswallow.

As she watched his progress, she decided that he was making the rounds of all the tables, offering some sort of announcement. When he got to their table, he smiled, not even a big smile, but Lucie felt a tangible punch to her solar plexus. Wow, that was weird. Must be the champagne. Maybe it had gone down the wrong way. So why did she still feel compelled to drop to the floor and check under his kilt?

Behave, she ordered herself.

"My dad asked me to stop by to make sure you're all enjoying yourselves," Ian offered. "I see you've got champagne, but the bar is also open—anything you want, courtesy of the Highland Inn. The waiters aren't going to start serving dinner for a while, though—the photographer is taking a few extra family pictures. But as nonfamily, you guys are off the hook, so you might as well have a few drinks, a dance, whatever."

He skimmed a quick glance around the table, long enough for Lucie to get a good glimpse of the color of his eyes. Blue. A beautiful, rich shade of blue that made her feel as if she'd just dived into the deep end of Lake Michigan. Or Loch Lomond. *You take the high road and I'll take the low road and I'll peek under your kilt on the wayyy...* She knocked back another glass of champagne.

But his gaze lit on her...and lingered.

"Wait," he said, and her heart felt as if it had stopped right there. Oh, she was waiting, all right. He narrowed his eyes. "I remember you from the rehearsal dinner. It's Lucie, isn't it?"

He knew her name? She was shocked. Especially since she'd been sitting about a football field away from him at the rehearsal dinner.

"Aren't you Steffi's sister?" he asked.

"Half sister," she corrected quickly.

"What's a half between friends?" He held out a hand. "I'll bet they're waiting for both of us, and I don't think your mother is a woman you want to leave hanging."

"Ginetta isn't my mother," Lucie said quickly. That should have been obvious—Steffi and her mother were both tiny in stature, barely five feet, with dark hair and eyes. At five nine, with wayward, wavy red hair and green eyes, Lucie wasn't even in the same ballpark. "Steffi and I... We share the same father."

"That still makes you part of the family." When she

didn't take his offered hand, he reached for hers, pulling her to her feet. "Come on, don't be shy. I don't want to have to come back for you. The faster we get this whole photo thing over with, the faster we can join the party."

We? What we? But she didn't have a chance to find out.

Stumbling along behind him, Lucie stared down at their joined hands, watched the pleats in his kilt frisk his well-shaped calves, gulped, blinked twice, shook her head, and gulped again. But he held on, steering them both across the ballroom and out the side door.

Uh-oh. What was wrong with her? For one thing, she'd shed her jacket and loosened her blouse, so she wasn't presentable for pictures. For another, she should've told him that no one would be champing at the bit, waiting for *her* to pose for family pictures.

She knew Steffi and Ginetta like the back of her hand, and they weren't going to like this. In their minds, there was Family—Dad, Ginetta and Steffi— and then there was the outsider, the nuisance, the nitwit—Lucie. She tried to get along with them, really she did. But they'd made it clear for years that she was *persona non grata.*

Ian pulled her behind him into a side room where a small cluster of people milled about, including the bride and groom. "Ian!" three different people cried at once.

"Ian, let's get a move on," the groom said impatiently. "Come on, we've been waiting for you."

"Hey, I completed my mission as fast as I could." He

smiled, dropping Lucie's hand, but then slid a casual arm around her. "Look, Steffi, I found your sister."

"*Half* sister," the two of them said automatically, as their mutual father, Donald Webster, started to get pink and fidgety, glancing between the bride and her mother as if he expected one or the other to blow sky-high.

A self-made man, he had a horror of looking tacky to those more sophisticated or higher up the social ladder, like the old-money Mackintosh family. Lucie recognized the symptoms—he always got that nervous shift to his eyes, those beads of sweat on his upper lip, when he felt outclassed.

There was an awkward silence.

"Excuse me. I'll just..." She'd never had any desire to annoy her father or put a crimp in Steffi's big day. So Lucie edged backward, ducking around Ian's arm and making for the door. "I'm sure Steffi wanted, you know, immediate family, and I'm sort of, well, *extended*."

"No, no, I'm sure—" Ian began. She heard his brother whisper, "Steffi? Don't you want your sister in the family pictures?" but the photographer was trying to push them into some sort of arrangement, and Lucie took her chance to escape.

She did pause for one extra second, however, long enough to watch the Mackintosh family pose as gracefully as you please, as if they had just stepped into an ad for greeting cards. They stood tall, exuding wealth and style. From the distinguished parents to their two elegant, fabulous sons and poised teenaged daughter, this family made a picture of perfection. And when they smiled, the whole room seemed to light up without any need for flashbulbs.

Wow. Lucie looked at them with real envy. No wonder Steffi wanted to marry into this family. It wasn't just that her groom was adorable and wonderful, rich and charming, although he certainly seemed to be. No, it was the whole family. They were perfect. But what would they want with Steffi?

None of her business, was it? She had a table full of wallflowers to get back to. As she slipped away into the reception, she heard the photographer behind her command, "And *smile!*"

IF ONE MORE PERSON told him to smile, Ian Mackintosh swore he'd start knocking heads together.

God, he hated weddings. Especially this one, with its boatload of pseudo-Scottish junk, outrageous number of bridesmaids, and way too many people smiling and pretending to be thrilled for Kyle.

Thrilled? Ha! His brother was making a huge mistake. Colossal. What else could you call it when a great guy like Kyle signed up for a life sentence with a twenty-one-year-old bimbo with a hot bod and the brains of a twig?

Ian wasn't that fond of the idea of marriage, anyway. As far as he was concerned, you traded a few minutes of pleasure for a lifetime of effort and commitment, boredom and compromise. He hated compromise. Even his parents, who looked like a flawless match on the outside, had had their share of ups and downs. It seemed like a full-time job for his dad to keep that marriage humming.

He loved his mother and his sister dearly, but they were often on some other planet he couldn't—and didn't really care to—understand. He just wasn't sure he could ever put that much work into something as mercurial and infuriating as a woman.

Besides, as he'd watched friends get married over the past few years, they'd so often seemed to be doing it for the wrong reasons—because somebody's parents were pushing it, or the girlfriend wanted a baby, or he was the right age, or she had a nice smile, or he was lonely, or all their friends were married...

It didn't take long for one or the other to be miserable. It didn't take long for Ian to run in the other direction. The merest hint of matrimony on the mind of a woman he was dating had him saying goodbye.

And he was even more convinced he was right now that he'd seen Steffi in action. Sure, he'd tried to give her the benefit of the doubt, and he'd been kind of amused by her sister, the sneezy redhead. At least *she* seemed like a real human being. But when he'd brought Lucie back for family pictures, snotty little Steffi had acted ruder than rude—to her own sister.

"Half sister," he said under his breath.

Fine. A bimbo, a social climber *and* a bitch, and she'd just married his brother. Wonderful.

What the hell was Kyle thinking, marrying Steffi? "She must be something special in the sack," he muttered, taking a long swig of his drink. Forget champagne. He'd turned to Scotch on the rocks a long time ago. Well, hey, at least it fit the theme.

"Ian, Ian, Ian, what are you doing all alone?" a silky female voice purred.

He glanced up. Ah, yes. The maid of honor. What was her name again?

The leggy blonde perched herself on the chair next to his. "Lucky I ran into you."

She'd apparently slipped upstairs to her room at the Inn long enough to change her clothes. All he had up in his room was an extra pair of jeans and a T-shirt to wear home tomorrow, or he would've gotten rid of his own kilt hours ago. But this nubile young thing had planned ahead, shedding her long wool skirt and hot jacket for a slinky little cocktail dress. He had to say, it looked good on her. And partially off her.

Although Ian was fully aware the maid of honor was cut from the same cloth as the bimbo bride, he also knew she could be useful for a few hours. She'd already telegraphed her interest, and then some. She might be feeling no pain at the moment, but she'd been perfectly sober when she tried to trap him in the coat room at the rehearsal dinner, and then pinched his butt as they walked out of the church after the ceremony.

The way he figured it, he was bummed and she and her bubble-headed beauty were a distraction. Where was the harm in that?

"Can I get you a drink, um...?" *Damn.* He really could not recall her name.

"Feather," she finished for him.

How could he have forgotten anything that silly? "Feather. Right. Let me get one of the waiters."

Feather downed several more Cosmopolitans (which was exactly what he would've guessed she'd drink) as she gossiped about Steffi and the other bridesmaids. "I think Steffi should've cut back to about five attendants and only picked the really good-looking ones, y'know?" She sat up straighter, only slightly wobbly. "A person has to have standards."

What was he supposed to say to that? *Sure, have all the standards you want. Who cares?* He raised his glass to his lips, preferring not to comment.

"Did you know that Steffi and I are soro... soror...sorory sisters?" She tried to get a grip on her drink, giggling when it sloshed over its rim and splashed red liquid onto the white linen tablecloth. "Oopsie! What was I saying? Oh, yeah—me and Steffi. We are just like *that.*" She squinted, trying to focus long enough to put her index fingers together. "Like *that.*"

"I got it."

Tipping over to one side, she propped herself up on an elbow. "You are so cute, y'know?"

"Uh, sure. Whatever." When she waited expectantly, he hastened to add, "And you, too. You're beautiful. But you already know that."

"Well, duh. Come on, don't I see myself in the mirror? Like, news flash."

Okay, not even for a few hours could he put up with this. He started to rise.

"Hey, where you goin'? Am I invited?"

He tried to remind himself that he wasn't looking for

conversation, just one night of guilt-free seduction, nothing too taxing, nothing too clingy, just fun and a few fireworks. What was he going to do otherwise? Go back to his room by himself, drink the other half of the bottle of Scotch, and fall into a depressed stupor. Yeah, that sounded enticing.

Feather gave him a sly wink, winding her tongue around a cherry she'd plucked from someone else's drink. After fooling with it for a few seconds, she popped it out of her mouth with the stem neatly tied in a knot. "Everybody has to have a talent," she giggled.

Ian sat back down.

"LUCIE," DELILAH ANNOUCNED, "I think we need to find some guys and fast. You and I—and especially you—need a fling."

"A fling?" By this time, Lucie had ditched her shoes under the table and rolled up her sleeves, and she was feeling much better. She'd also switched from champagne to strawberry margaritas, and she swirled sugar onto her tongue while she considered her fellow bridesmaid's idea. "You mean like a one-night stand? Why exactly do I need that?"

"Dying on the vine, my dear. Dying on the vine. I mean, here we are, bridesmaids at this big, ugly ol' wedding with a million guys running around, and what are we doing? Talking to each other." Delilah shook her head sadly. "We need to get out there and find us some guys. You know, for overnight. Or maybe not even overnight, just a couple of hours. Heck, just a couple of minutes!"

"You are *so* bad," Lucie returned in a stage whisper. She said with determination, "If I'm doing it, I'm not settling for a couple of minutes. Not tonight."

"You go, girl!"

"Darn right." Lucie lifted her chin. "Did I tell you it's my birthday? And not just any birthday. The big 3-0."

Delilah's mouth dropped open. "Get out! You're thirty? Today? Okay, now I know I'm right. Lucie, honey, you are in dire need of a little nookie, a little fun, some snap and crackle, y'know? I mean, good grief."

"I don't know...."

"Oh, come on!" Delilah's speech picked up speed and volume as she gained enthusiasm. "Go for it! Have a fling! You'll never turn thirty again. Besides, you're a bridesmaid. It's what bridesmaids do. Look around you—everyone is pairing up."

Through the mist of a few too many alcoholic beverages, Lucie surveyed the rapidly thinning crowd in the ballroom. "Oh, my god. You're right. There are trysts forming before my very eyes!"

In fact, directly in her line of vision, she saw Ian, the handsome best man, sitting very close to Steffi's maid of honor, the one with the silicone-inflated cleavage and legs up to her chin. From here, it looked as if the two of them were getting cozy. *Very* cozy. Yuck.

And if she looked the other way, her gaze hit snippy little Steffi, out on the dance floor in her white lace wedding dress, clinging to her handsome groom like there was no tomorrow.

Steffi, twenty-one and married to a drop-dead gorgeous guy in his thirties. Her hideous maid of honor, also twenty-something, also attached to a gorgeous guy in his thirties.

And here sat Lucie, thirty and alone. "Well," she said with spirit, "isn't *that* a kick in the pants?"

As IAN TRIED to decide where he was going with this, Feather made her move. Bending in close enough to give him a full view of her dangerously round breasts, she slid a hand onto his knee, teasing the edge of his kilt. She whispered, "Are you feeling what I'm feeling?"

"What are you feeling?"

"Hot. Hot, hot, hot."

He smiled. Okay, so he was human, and when a woman put her hand under his kilt, he had the obvious reaction. "Maybe."

"I know you're as turned on as I am," she mouthed. "Tell you what—just give me your key, and we'll take this upstairs." As he made no move, she pouted and tried, "Come on, Ian. Everybody knows the best man and the maid of honor are supposed to make it on the wedding night. It's kind of a..." She winked at him. "A tradition."

He told himself not to be an idiot. She might not be the swiftest boat in the fleet, but Feather was a beautiful, willing, sexy woman. Was he really going to turn her down?

Not on your life. He reached into his jacket pocket and pulled out the key. The number 2-0-3 caught the light of a nearby candle as he slipped it across the table.

Feather offered a triumphant smile, nabbing the key and sticking it quickly into the small plaid handbag looped around her wrist. "You go ahead," she said in a breathy voice. "I'll just freshen up and then I'll be right with you."

As she toddled off in the direction of the ladies' room, Ian pondered the odds of her actually making it up the stairs to his room. Fifty-fifty, he decided. But hey, that was like letting fate decide whether a horizontal tango with Feather was meant to be.

He grabbed the bottle of Scotch on the table, stopped by the front desk for another key to his room, and strolled up to the second floor, still in a very dark and cynical frame of mind.

If Feather made the climb or if she didn't, it was no big deal to him.

"IT'S WHAT HAPPENS at weddings, Luce. It's like they pump something into the air. All the sexual tension, the weepy till-death-do-us-part stuff, everyone thinking about honeymoons and garters and sloppy kisses and white lace and roses and... Well, the open bar doesn't hurt, either."

"Okay, so everyone else is doing it. That doesn't mean I have to," Lucie protested. "I'm just not that kind of person." She hiccuped delicately. "Besides, my father would have a fit."

"What's he got to do with it?" Delilah argued. "And why would he even have to know?"

"He wouldn't, I suppose. It's just...he's very hung

up on toeing the line, not making waves, not doing anything that would embarrass him."

"Let me get this straight. This is the same man whose daughter just foisted this Scottish monstrosity of a wedding on about four hundred people?" Delilah shook her head so hard she looked dizzy. "Lucie, you are thirty years old. What your father does or doesn't like is hardly important at this point—especially when the old jerk let Steffi have her wedding on your birthday."

"Oh, I'm sure none of them remembered. It's not like it was intentional," Lucie assured her new friend.

"That's even worse."

"Not really—"

"I'm telling you, Luce," Delilah interrupted. "Tonight, for a few hours, you deserve to think about *you*, to celebrate the big 3-0, to be as wild and wicked as you've always wanted to be."

Still, Lucie hesitated.

The other bridesmaid demanded, "Come on, Lucie, what are you afraid of?"

What *was* she afraid of?

"Don't be shy—don't even think about it," Delilah counseled. "After all, it's no biggie." There was a spark of mischief in her smile. "Just a harmless little fling."

2

JUST A LITTLE FLING.

It might not sound scary to Delilah, but it was like jumping off a cliff to Lucie.

"I don't know if I can," she hedged. But a tiny, reckless voice inside her whispered, *You know you want to.* "I—I don't know."

"Which is exactly why you're sitting here by yourself on your birthday, with nobody warm and friendly to curl up to." Delilah pushed herself to her feet. "Harsh words, my dear, but true. Don't look now, but my best shot at my own fling is heading for the bar, and I think I can intercept him. Paolo has my name written all over him."

With a determined glint in her eye, Delilah stalked off in search of big game.

"Paolo?" Lucie muttered, squinting after Delilah. "Who is Paolo? Oh, good heavens. It's the cranky busboy."

Dejected, Lucie watched the candle flame sputter into a wisp of smoke in front of her. The bride and groom had left. Ian and his bimbo had left. Delilah was hot on the trail of a busboy. And Lucie was alone at her table.

Alone on her thirtieth birthday. This was just *wrong*.

"I'm going to do it," she said suddenly. Fortifying herself by chugging the last of her margarita, Lucie stood up and unsteadily surveyed the ballroom. "Who's it going to be?"

She frowned, weighing the prospects. It couldn't be just anyone. Her head might be buzzing with champagne and tequila, but she still wasn't stupid enough to put the moves on just anybody. Nobody with a wedding ring. Nobody who looked too old or too young or too...scary.

But then who? Shaking her head from side to side, Lucie tried to clear her mind enough to make a rational decision. Not that there was anything rational about any of this.

It's my birthday, the brash, foolhardy side of her brain argued. *You didn't get even one present. You deserve this!*

Okay, okay. The fling was on. So who was the lucky guy?

There was a relatively cute guy over by the dance floor giving her the eye, but he looked kind of strange. Or maybe just a little too eager.

And then there was Baker Burns.

Good old Baker. Feeling sentimental all of a sudden, Lucie smiled. He gave her a friendly wave from the cake table, where he was casually eating dessert, not a care in the world. He, too, was all by himself. Hmm... Okay, so he wasn't terribly exciting. But he was safe, and that seemed like a good idea at the moment. Safe, predictable, boring Baker Burns...

"He's perfect," she whispered. All she wanted was one night of—what had Delilah called it?—nookie.

One night of nookie. No future. No trouble. Just one night. Who else *but* Baker Burns fit that bill?

So she grabbed her tartan purse, the useless little thing Steffi had given them all as bridesmaid's presents, and padded purposefully to the cake table.

"Hello, Baker," she began, working hard to keep that breathless, tipsy tremble out of her voice.

"Hiya, Luce," he said calmly, holding up a plate in each hand. "Did you want white or chocolate? Don't worry—only the icing is plaid."

Naturally he assumed she was trolling for extra wedding cake. "Oh, no. None for me, thanks." As he set down the plates, she forged ahead, determined to be bold. What did vampy, flirty girls do in these situations? Maybe a little eyelash batting? "Having a good time, Baker?" she inquired coyly, leaning in nearer and flapping her lashes to beat the band.

He'd turned away to retrieve his own cake, but he stopped, his fork in midair. With concern, he asked, "Is there something wrong with your eye?"

Oh, hell. Eyelash batting was a bust.

"Listen, Baker," she said, coming right out with it, "I'm by myself, you're by yourself, and it's my birthday. I was wondering whether you were interested in getting together tonight. You and me."

"You? A-a-and me?" It sounded as if a hunk of cake had lodged in his windpipe. He choked, "D-did you just...?"

"Right. You and me. What do you say?" When he still couldn't manage to get out any words, Lucie snapped, "Come on, I haven't got all day. Do you want to sleep with me or not?"

Baker's eyebrows rose past his receding hairline. "Are you drunk?"

"Heavens, no." Lucie paused, wondering if the cake behind Baker was really tilting or her eyesight had gone wacky. Best not to think about it. "Well, maybe I've had a little more to drink than normal," she admitted. "But that's not what this is about. I'm serious, Baker. What do you think about a wedding-night fling with an old friend?"

"Y-yes. Sure! Now? Do you want to leave now?"

"Yes, I want to leave now. Right this minute." *Before I lose my tequila-induced nerve.*

"Okay." He paused, carefully placing his plate back on the table behind him. Taking a deep breath, he peered at her, as if he couldn't quite believe what was happening. She knew the feeling. "Where? I mean, your room or mine? I mean, you do want to go to a room, right? You don't have fantasies about, like, the 18th green or a phone booth or the hood of a Corvette or something, do you?"

Lucie's mouth dropped open. Clearly, there was more to Baker than she'd realized. Eighteenth green? Phone booth? Hood of a Corvette? She swallowed. "Actually, I was thinking of a, uh, bed."

A bed. Good lord. *Bed.* She'd no more said the word than hazy, smoky images assailed her. Images of sheets tangled around sweaty, naked skin. Pillows and blankets scattered to the four winds in reckless, passionate abandon. Springs squeaking in protest as bodies thrashed above them. And a man, pressed so close she could hear his heartbeat, feel his heat, touch his...

Baker cleared his throat. "Um, Lucie?"

She jumped, wobbling onto one foot, as her erotic reverie ended in a hurry. *Get a grip,* she told herself curtly, fanning herself with the miniature handbag. *We're talking Baker here. Forget tangled sheets and mad passion. This is Baker.*

"Listen..." He wiped his brow with the back of one hand, reaching into the pocket of his jacket with the other. "About the room thing. Mine's fine, if you want to. I mean, I'm in..." he peered at his key. "...uh, 302. Where are you?"

She glanced at the brass key in his hand. Curving script that read *Highland Inn* was etched into the metal, and then the number *302.* "You mean Steffi put you up here, in the Inn?"

Oh, sure! *Baker* had a room at the Inn. Probably every single member of the wedding party except Lucie got to stay right here. But her? Not even close. "I'm in some junky motel halfway to Wisconsin," she told him with more than a touch of annoyance. "I'm not even checked in yet."

"Uh, right." Baker blinked. "Well, it doesn't sound like we want to have our, uh, liaison there. So I guess it's my room then. You know, if you want to give me a few minutes, I could go on up and arrange some champagne and candles and stuff. That might be nice."

Lucie barely heard him. She was still seething over the way Steffi managed to diss her, even when it came to a hotel. He awkwardly handed her the key, and without thinking, she grabbed it and dropped it into the bottom of her tiny purse.

"All right then," he told her, his words tumbling over each other. "But I want you to know, if you change your mind, I won't hold it against you. I'll just wait, oh, I don't know, a half hour, and if you're not there, I'll blow out the candles and forget it ever happened. Okay?"

"Right. Half an hour." And then she realized what she'd done. She'd just taken Baker's key. They had made an official...assignation.

It's not too late to back out, the timid half of her brain put in. *Are you really sure you want to do this?*

But Baker was already scooting off to the stairs, sending her encouraging glances over his shoulder.

"Baker," she called out, "about what you said, about how I might need to, maybe, I don't know, reserve the right to, you know..."

Change my mind? But he was gone.

"What have I done?" Lucie cried. With the ribbon ties on her purse clutched in both hands, she swung one way and then the other, looking for something in the room that would give her courage or help her make up her mind. "The ladies' room!"

She had no idea why that would help, but it always seemed to. The few times she'd been on rotten dates and she was trying to decide whether to bolt or stick it out, a trip to the rest room had been really comforting, really useful. She could splash cool water on her face, sit down for a sec, give herself time to think. At the very least, she could loosen her uncomfortable skirt and get a little more blood flowing.

"A time-out is just what I need," she decided, making a beeline for the ladies' room out in the hall on the other side of the ballroom.

She pushed open the door in a rush, giving herself a pep talk and not really paying attention to much else. Momentarily blinded by a cloud of perfume and hair spray, she almost collided with the same giggly blonde she'd seen sticking her hands under Ian Mackintosh's kilt earlier, Steffi's insipid, snobby maid of honor, the one with the stupid name. Flora? Fauna? No, more like Finger. Flicker?

Whatever her name, she was exactly the person Lucie did *not* want to run into.

"Would you watch where you're going?" the girl snarled. "What a klutz." Only it came out more like *klush*. With a huff, she turned back to the process of peering at herself in the mirror over the sink, attempting to add another layer of lipstick to already over-glossed lips.

One look and Lucie could tell that the maid of honor was sloshed to the gills. Maybe it was the flushed cheeks or the drooping eyelids or the slurred speech. Or the way the girl's head bobbled back and forth as she tried to focus on keeping the lipstick remotely inside her lipline.

"Isn't that attractive?" Lucie muttered.

"Can I borrow that?" another twenty-something chirped, popping up at the first one's elbow. "It's mocha cocoa muck, isn't it? I love that color on you, Feather."

Oh, right. Feather. Worse than Flora or Fauna.

"It is not mocha cocoa muck. It's Poisonberry Smog. It's all I ever wear. And no, you cannot borrow it," Feather returned, giving herself another thick coat of the stuff, smacking her lips at the mirror. "I need it. All of it. I want to leave marks all over him." She swung one arm wide, almost hitting her friend. With a smirk, she added, "Three days from now, Ian Mackintosh is still going to be finding traces of Poisonberry Smog."

Lucie narrowed her eyes. The idea of Feather applying Poisonberry lip-prints all over Ian Mackintosh was too disgusting to contemplate.

And then the blonde made it even worse. Giggling, she trotted over to a small machine attached to the wall, started spinning the crank, and scooped little multicolored packets out of it like there was no tomorrow. "Free condoms!" she cooed. "And I plan to use every single one of them."

"Excuse me, but don't you think you should leave some for the rest of us?" Lucie interrupted, skirting around the sink and honing in. "I think the machine is there as a courtesy, not for your private stock."

"Oh, yeah, like you expect me to believe *you* need one. Puh-leez." Her nose in the air, Feather tossed about ten of them into her plaid minibag and closed the drawstring with a vicious jerk.

Really starting to get ticked off here, Lucie grabbed a handful herself, whipped out her own identical purse, and shoved in the rainbow assortment of small squares. She made a point of yanking her ribbons, too, with the same show of force. Only she yanked too hard and the whole purse went flying, like a slingshot, smacking Feather in the right eye.

"Oh, my God!" Feather howled, dropping her bag, strewing condoms and cosmetics every which way as she covered her injured eye. "She tried to kill me!"

"I'm so sorry," Lucie tried immediately, hovering there. "Are you all right?"

"Do I look all right? I'm probably blind, you idiot!" She began to wail loudly, as her friend attempted to pry her fingers away.

"Feather, I think it looks okay. Really." The other girl bent to gather the scattered items. "Your lipstick rolled under the sink, but I got it. Don't move, because the blush and mascara and stuff are right by your foot. Where's your purse?" She glanced between the two matching plaid bags lying side by side on the floor. "Which one is which?"

"No problem. We'll just look inside. I think this one is mine," Lucie said awkwardly, reaching for the closest purse. She opened it quickly, finding seven or eight condoms and a Highland Inn key right on top. Yeah, that's what should be in her purse. But just to be sure, she pulled out the key. "Room 203," she read. That was what she recalled Baker had said.

"Give me my purse!" Feather cried tearfully. "If that's yours, I want mine. With all my stuff in it. I need to fix my eye. My mascara is running!"

"I put everything back. It's fine," the friend said

soothingly. "Look, here's your makeup and your room key and, see, I'm putting all your condoms back..."

Deciding a quick exit was in everyone's best interests, Lucie got out of there, clasping the small tartan bag securely to her chest. But where was she going to go?

The reception hall was almost empty as she passed through. It seemed everyone had either paired up or gone home. Walking slowly into the front hall, Lucie hesitated. It had started to rain again during the reception, and she could hear the steady pitter-patter of the downpour against the windows.

On one side was the main door, leading to the outside world. On the other was the big double staircase leading to the second floor and the hotel part of the Inn.

Which way? Should she march out the front door into the rain, find the parking lot and her car, and drive an hour to that cut-rate motel in the middle of nowhere when she'd been drinking? Or should she pull out the key to room 203, climb the stairs, and have her cozy little rendezvous with Baker Burns?

She'd been over all the reasons she wanted to do this, all about her neglected birthday and her nine-years-younger sister marrying the perfect man and now poor Baker up there with champagne, depending on her, and her in no condition to drive... She licked her lip, gazing around at the Highland Inn, at the flickering candles casting a romantic glow on the soft stone walls and that wide, inviting, dangerous staircase.

"Lucie, are you a woman or a worm?" she asked out loud. "You're not a child, you're not a virgin, and you have condoms. What more do you need? Lightning bolts?"

As if some cosmic force had heard her words, there was a huge clap of thunder, and the front hall lit up with the slash of accompanying lightning. Lucie jumped about a foot.

"Okay, so I got the lightning bolt."

A rushing sound filled her ears, as she stumbled up the stairs, one hand stuck to the heavy wooden railing and the other clutching the key. "What's that number again?" she murmured, squinting down into her hand as she hit the landing. "Was it 302? No, 203." Bad time to turn dyslexic. Maybe she was just nervous.

Nervous? No, she was petrified!

But lo and behold, there was room 203 right in front of her. She tiptoed up, she slid the key into the hole, and easy as you please, the door yawned open.

Her heart pounding, the rushing sound getting louder, Lucie took one step inside. Inky blackness greeted her.

So much for candles and champagne. She must not have made it upstairs within the allotted time. Poor Baker must've decided not to wait. That was okay. In her newfound boldness, she would simply wake him. In a way, it was less scary like this. She would strip off her clothes, climb in with him, and ease them both into this fling thing.

Lucie paused, waiting for her eyes to adjust, but it didn't help much. She could make out a large, square blob directly ahead, with a few other indistinct shapes looming here and there. A canopy bed, maybe, with curtains pulled around it. And a desk? There was no light coming in at all to relieve the unrelenting darkness.

"Baker?" she whispered.

No answer. Had she said his name out loud or only thought it? If only she hadn't drunk so much champagne and knocked back all those margaritas. If only her brain were functioning.

But if she hadn't, or if it were, she wouldn't be here, would she?

She took another step. Her stocking foot slid on a pile of fabric lying right in her path. Although it gave her a moment of panic when she began to slip, she caught herself and then stood still for a second, trying to refocus her swimming head. Peering down, she also identified the nubby wool still cloaking her foot. A kilt. A black-and-red Mackintosh tartan, just like all the groomsmen had been wearing. Baker's kilt.

Okay, that wasn't so frightening, was it? Exhaling a nervous puff of air, Lucie bent to quietly drop her purse and take off her boots. Oh, she wasn't wearing any. Where had they gotten off to? She didn't remember doffing her shoes, but she supposed she must've. Maybe she'd left them downstairs in the reception hall with her jacket. Oh well.

At least her hideous kneesocks were easy to peel away, even if she was a bit uncoordinated at the moment. But it felt great to be free of the nasty things. She flexed her bare toes, beaming into the dark room.

Picking up steam, she reached for the waistband of her skirt, but her fingers were clumsy and she couldn't get the complicated little fasteners to work. "The hell with it," she swore under her breath, popping hooks and buckles as she tore off the skirt, letting it pool at her feet on top of the groomsman's kilt.

Ah, that felt like heaven. She could breathe again! She wanted to dance on it, stomp it into the carpet.

Now all she had to do was get rid of the rest of her confining clothes. Impatient, she ripped off her blouse, her panties and bra, throwing them carelessly aside. *I am a wild woman, hear me roar!* she sung inside her head. *Happy birthday to me!*

Swinging her head, she undid the neat bun, releasing the full length of her red-gold hair to flow freely over her shoulders. Paradise!

And now she was ready. Nothing left to do but...

Wait a second. She scampered back to where she'd discarded her purse, pulling out one of the bright packets from the machine and closing her hand around it. Best to be prepared. Not that she and Baker were necessarily going to do that, anyway, but that was the idea, wasn't it? If she got in with him wearing nothing but a smile, she had to expect a certain level of, well, intimacy.

So... She extracted another foil square, clutching it in her hand with the first one. You never knew.

Her heart was in her throat as she crept closer to the heavily draped four-poster. She slipped her free hand inside the curtain, feeling for anything. She thought she could hear him breathing.

The rhythm of his breath grew rougher, more ragged, as her hand closed on warm, smooth skin. Oh, yeah, he was in there. The wooden bedframe squeaked as he moved nearer her hand.

This was no time to be shy. Leaning inside the dark bed curtain, Lucie balanced one knee on the mattress. And her fingers stretched further, sliding over the firm ridges of his ribs, the strong expanse of his muscled torso. Her gulp sounded like a gong in the silent room.

"Is that you?" she whispered, in a raspy, strange voice.

But she knew, even before the words left her mouth, that there was no way in hell that chest belonged to safe, reliable Baker Burns.

What was worse, she didn't care.

His hand closed over her wrist, grabbing her, pulling her off balance, hauling her all the way through the curtains and into the bed. She didn't even try to regain her equilibrium, just went with the flow, sliding up his body, taking in the hard, slippery, intoxicating feel of him against her skin. A moan of pure bliss escaped her lips. Had she ever felt pleasure like this? Not a chance.

Closing her eyes, she pressed closer, fitting herself to his long, lean body, rubbing just enough to make herself tingle from head to toe. So this was what a fling felt like. Like one big beautifully wrapped package that she got to keep opening all night long.

Lucie smiled wickedly into the darkness. *Oh, yeah. Happy birthday to me.*

IAN KNEW THE SECOND he touched her that this was no Feather. His brain was hazy and polluted by Scotch fumes, but not oblivious enough to mistake a living, breathing, vivacious *woman* for a pale imitation like Feather.

Was he dreaming? But her skin and her curves felt warm, vibrant, incredibly real—too real to be either Feather or a dream.

So who was she and where did she come from? He peered at her in the dim light, but her features were obscured by a long fall of hair, and he knew he'd never seen this body before. Who was she? His mind was foggy enough and his body turned on enough not to complain.

As the long tendrils of her silky hair rippled over his shoulder and his chest, he felt small sparks of desire in its wake. He leaned back, giving in to the sensations. But the way she was wiggling against him, her hips meeting his, was already making him feel like a rocket, ready to launch, and he knew he had to slow it down. Fast.

He reached for her, arching up, filling his hands with her hair, finding her sweet, wet mouth and plunging inside. God, she tasted good.

Even better, she kissed him back hard, hungrily, ferociously, making more of those greedy little noises that were driving him insane. She was nibbling and sliding, tasting and rubbing, climbing all over him in her eagerness. He grinned against her mouth. It just didn't get any better than this.

With one swift motion, he rolled her underneath him, pinning her hands at her sides. She whimpered, edging up into him, teasing him with the feel of her soft, full breasts brushing his chest. He held himself rigid. "Whoever you are, lady, I want you. I want you bad. But are you sure this is what you want?"

"Positive," she said breathlessly. Slowly, she opened her hand, the one she'd been holding in a tight little fist, revealing two small, opaque packets, one red and one blue. "See? I came prepared."

Ian laughed out loud. "You hang onto those," he murmured, bending down to press his lips into the slope of her neck, enjoying the unsteady pulse that throbbed there, the way she panted and shivered when he kissed her. "We'll get to them."

Either her buttons were remarkably easy to push, or she was very aroused. He knew the feeling. Already, she was restless and impatient under him, but he had no intention of rushing anything or giving her what she obviously wanted.

Instead, he backed off, barely grazing her shoulder with his mouth before he held himself away. His lids lowered as he gazed down at her. Beautiful. Whoever she was, this naked goddess who'd come calling, she was long and lithe, curvy and luscious, with pale, porcelain skin that glowed even in this faint light and a riot of hair spilling out in every direction.

Ian smiled. Yeah, this was going to take a while.

WHY DIDN'T HE hurry up? She was dying down here. Lucie groaned with frustration, writhing near the edge of the bed. She was melting from the inside out, and she didn't think she could be any more wet, hot, ready. His clever, versatile mouth showed no mercy on her breasts and her belly, teasing her, biting and swirling, pushing her into this mindless, dazzled, semiconscious place, where all she did was ache for him, hate him, wait for him, *want* him.

Why did he have to move so damn slowly?

Finally, just when she thought she might expire from this terrible need, he slid lower. Lucie gasped. If she'd thought his tongue was skillful before, now she knew what it could really do. It could make her weep with pleasure. It could bring her hurtling to the top so fast she saw stars.

She'd never been like this before, every inch of her humming and shattering, where every flick of his tongue brought her higher, faster, harder.

"Oh, yessss," she cried. "Don't stop. Don't...*stop!*" But she was already peaking, falling and peaking again. She melted into a puddle of satisfaction, curling into him. "Don't stop..."

He lifted his head. His low, heated voice coiled around her like flame when he whispered, "Don't worry. We're just getting started."

"I think," she murmured in a husky, vixenish voice she didn't recognize as her own, "now it's your turn."

She opened her fist again, sparing a moment to stuff the still unused condoms under the pillow for safe-keeping.

"Maybe later," she whispered, sliding down his flank, twisting herself around him.

"Maybe later," he echoed.

But first...

MORNING LIGHT drifted slowly into the room, casting a soft, warm glow on Lucie.

She opened one eye. "Mmmph," she mumbled, unable to recognize the fuzzy shapes in front of her.

Stretching out an arm, yawning, she blinked, opening both eyes. A draft tickled her shoulders, making her quite certain she wasn't wearing a top. Or a bottom.

Naked. In a high, soft bed she didn't recognize, with intricately carved posts and thick draperies cascading down from the edges of the canopy overhead.

Taking silent inventory, she noted that there seemed to be a pillow wedged under her stomach, and her head, most of her hair, and one arm were hanging off the bed, dangling in space. An assortment of rumpled bedclothes had been tossed onto the floor below her, and a rainbow of small, ripped packets, red and blue and green and yellow, lay scattered around them.

Those were condom packets, she realized with sudden alarm. She counted. Six empty condom packets. Six?

What did that mean?

As she lifted her chin, she thought she could hear someone breathing behind her. Not only that, but she could feel hot puffs of air on her back, just below her shoulder blade, and an unfamiliar weight, as if someone were lying there, his head in the middle of her back, breathing on her.

What in blazes...?

Uh-oh. Things were starting to come back to her. Bad things.

She was getting fragments, strange shards of memory. And her head hurt. She tried to concentrate. What did these bizarre thoughts mean? Something about the reception and some nutty woman telling her she really ought to have a fling. And then Baker and a key and an idiotic blonde in the bathroom, and she'd crept up the stairs and into a dark room...

But this couldn't be Baker. Not the way her body felt all rubbed down, stoked up, worked out and trampled on, as if it had danced the tango to hell and back. More than once. She tried to move a few muscles. *Yeow*. Exactly what did they do?

She had these vague memories of her bed partner, of being upside down and on top of him, under him, on the floor, half on and half off the bed, of pretty much acting like a Flying Wallenda without a trapeze. That all had to be some erotic fantasy, right? People didn't really do those things.

"Okay, you're fine," she whispered to herself. "Probably you had too much to drink and you fell into a stupor in some guy's bed. Probably you were both too drunk to perform and nothing happened."

Comforting, but hardly realistic given the aftershocks still humming through her nervous system. Not to mention all those empty condom packets.

"Well," she continued, trying not to panic, "whatever you did, he did it, too. Whoever he is."

Quietly, carefully, trying not to fall into hysteria, she eased herself back into the bed all the way, craning her neck so she could see who was back there, breathing on her. He rolled away from her, freeing her, and she saw dark hair, a beautifully sculpted torso, broad shoulders... She could just make out the side of his face, but a picture fell into her muddled brain with a clunk. A picture of her half sister standing at the altar, beaming up at a face just like this one.

"Oh, my god!" she screamed, bolting upright, clutching the pillow to her front. "I slept with the groom!"

"The groom? Who? Wha...?" He jumped awake all at once, sitting up stark naked, staring at her. "I'm not the groom. I swear. But who are you?"

"Wait, wait, wait." Keeping an arm secure around her protective pillow, she lifted a weak hand to her brow, shoving back a wall of hair, wishing her head would stop pounding like that. The whole room seemed to be beating like a drum. Or was that just her heart? Why did it have to be so loud?

"Who are you? And why are you shouting?"

"I remember you now," Lucie ventured slowly. *Breathe in. Breathe out.* It could be worse. She remembered him. He wasn't the groom. He was handsome. He was nice. It could be a lot worse. If only he weren't quite so naked. She bent down over the edge, grabbed a sheet, and flung it back up on the bed. "If you don't mind, could you please, you know, cover up?"

His jaw clenched. But he took it. With a grim expression, he looped the fine linen over his lap. "Better?"

"Yes, thank you." Still unwilling to look directly at him, Lucie compulsively rubbed her finger over the intricate carvings in the dark wood post beside her. "As I said, I remember you. You're right—you're not the groom. You're the best man, Ian. You were supposed to have lip prints all over you from Feather. I was supposed to find Baker and have my one night of nookie. I think we got our wires crossed."

"Huh?"

Losing it, Lucie bridged the gap between them, took him by the shoulders, and shook him. Hard. "What the hell were we thinking? How did this happen? And how did it happen *six* times?"

Wincing, Ian peeled her hands off his shoulders. "You just dropped your pillow."

Her body flushed with hot color as she let loose with a particularly colorful curse word and smacked him with the full brunt of the stupid pillow. Then, with dignity, she reattached it to her front and stretched out her other hand behind her to find something more reliable. But there was nothing to find. The heavy coverlet was pooled on the floor, nowhere near her.

"Sit still," he said darkly, leaning over her, spreading out his sheet to cover her, too. "There. That ought to do it."

Delicately clasping it up to her neck, Lucie huddled on her side of the bed, not touching any of him.

"I just... I haven't got a clue how we ended up together," he said gingerly. But he extended a finger, gently lifting a tendril of her hair as he smiled encouragingly. "Do we know each other?"

"Well, actually, yes. After last night, I think it's fair to say we know each other intimately." She concentrated on bringing air into her lungs. Calmly. Slowly. No need to hyperventilate. Also no need for a mental slide show of the level of that intimacy. "But we did meet before that—you came to my table and you dragged me over to be in the family picture. Ring any bells?"

"Kind of," he murmured slowly. "But how did we get from there…to *here?*"

"I don't know. I really don't know. Baker gave me a key. Room 302. I came right here."

"But this is 203."

"Isn't that what I said? Oh. This is 203? Then he must be in 302. But why would his key work in your door?" She shook her head, grabbing her hair in one hand and twisting it into a knot just to get it out of her way. "I don't understand."

"The hair. I remember you now. Lucie, the sneezy redhead." He rammed a hand into his forehead. "Steffi's sister. Oh, lord. What have we done?"

That was the ten-million-dollar question, wasn't it?

3

IAN'S HEAD FELT like a bongo drum. He knew he had a massive hangover, but that wasn't the half of it.

He had just slept with Lucie Webster. And he was in big trouble.

For one thing, she was not at all his type. Sure, they'd hit it off big-time in the sack. But he could tell just by looking she was too bright, too interesting, too challenging, way too six-kids-and-a-house-in-the-suburbs. One glance at her and he saw his future stretching before him, full of lace curtains and hand-thrown pots, salt-and-pepper-shaker collections, *New York Times* crossword puzzles, and schmaltzy black-and-white movies on video. And that was a best-case scenario. *Yechhhh.*

She was also not the kind of woman who was satisfied with a one-night stand, which was exactly why she wasn't the kind of woman he wanted. She had trust and respect and commitment written all over her.

As well as some bodacious curves. *Ian, keep your mind on trust, respect and commitment—all the things you avoid with a vengeance.*

Even worse than that, she came straight from the same grasping, social-climbing family as the petulant princess who'd just shackled his poor brother. For all he knew, this was the way Steffi got her foot in Kyle's door. And the last thing he needed was to step into the same quicksand that was trapping Kyle.

Ian tried to sort out how to get out of this mess with even a scrap of self-respect, but every time he tried to think, he kept getting this loud echo inside his brain. Boom, boom, boom. He vaguely remembered a bottle of Scotch with his name on it. That would explain the rock band in his head.

"Listen, can you call down to room service and get some coffee up here?" he asked in a very soft voice, trying to avoid the damn echo. It didn't work.

"No, I cannot call room service," the woman in his bed yelled. Well, maybe she didn't really yell. Maybe it only seemed like yelling. "If I call room service, they will know I'm here, won't they? I don't want anyone to know I'm here, and especially not some nice, wide-eyed kid who's going to roll his cart in here and then run back to Room Service Central to tell everyone that he saw you and me and six empty condom packages. Six!"

He was sorry he'd asked. "We could clean up the floor before he got here. Did you say six?" He didn't mean to smile. Lord knew, this was nothing to smile about. "Six, huh?"

"I'm glad that news cheers one of us up."

"I'm sorry," he offered before he knew what he was saying. He *was* sorry. It's just that apologizing wasn't necessarily the tactic he would've chosen if he'd had his wits about him. "Lucie, I don't know what to say. I

wish I remembered more about what happened or
what we did..."

But he did remember. All of a sudden, the memories
came flooding back with startling detail. Good God.

His gaze rocketed over to her, skidded off, and
landed somewhere on the foot of the bed. Could he really have...? Could she really have...? She sure didn't
seem like the type. He wasn't sure *he* was the type.
Good God. He actually felt like blushing. He hadn't
blushed since he was twelve.

And right now, he had to be out of that bed and
more than a few inches away from Lucie Webster. He
was starting to sweat from the flashbacks.

"Okay, listen." He jumped out from under the sheet
and deftly whipped the heavy side curtain from the
bed around his flanks as he turned. "Probably we need
to talk about this, but I think maybe a shower is what I
need. Unless..." He gave her a short glance. "You
first?"

"I am not going to get naked in *your* shower," she returned hotly, as if his shower was any more intimate
than what they'd already done. As if anything in the
universe was more intimate than what they'd already
done.

The shower. *Oh, hell.* Ian leaned his head against the
hard wood of the bedpost. The shower was where
they'd ended up during round six of their no-holds-
barred wrestling match, unless he was very much mistaken. The kaleidoscope of pictures unfolding in his
brain told him he was not mistaken.

There they all were, in blinding clarity. One was on

the bed with her on top; two was half-off the bed with him behind; three was on the floor, sort of a continuation of two after they rested for a minute; four was back on the bed but he was on top, and five was on the desk.

And six...up against the wall of the shower, with the water on full blast.

He squeezed his eyes closed but the pictures remained. His only hope of sanity was that Lucie didn't remember.

"All right," he said darkly, "then why don't you get dressed while I take a shower?" He'd just have to keep his eyes shut, point the other way and make the water really cold. *Really* cold.

"Why don't I leave? Like, immediately." Lucie scooted out the side of the bed in a wave of cream-colored linen wrapped toga-style. "I'll just get my clothes..." She kicked at the pile of tartans on the floor, frowning as she held up her skirt in one hand. "It's all ripped. All down the side. I guess I was in a...hurry." Looking even more dazed than before, she took a deep breath. "No buttons on my blouse, either. This is great. This is just great. I suppose I could tie the blouse on, but then what do I do below the waist? You don't have about ten safety pins, do you?"

"No." Was she crazy or was he? Safety pins?

"Great," she repeated, even crankier this time. "I have no clothes, not a stitch, and I'm stuck in a hotel room with Mr. Sleeps-With-Anything-That-Moves of Greater Chicagoland—"

"That's hardly fair," he put in, although it was difficult to argue while wearing half a bed curtain, while his mind and body still rocked with erotic aftershocks. "You don't know who I sleep with."

He stretched out a toe, trying to snag the bedspread. He also worked on kicking the empty condom wrappers under the bed, since they seemed to be bothering Lucie so much.

"I don't?" she asked angrily. "Aside from me, who happens to be a virtual stranger, you mean?"

She was busy wiggling into her panties while hanging onto her sheet, and the suggestive motions didn't do his temperature any good. Much better idea for him to play soccer with condom packages and ignore her.

"And why would I think you sleep around?" she went on. "Hmm... I wonder."

He held himself very still, hoping she wasn't going to mention anything about the floor or the shower or the energetic tango half-off the bed. God, that one was *magnificent*. Kinky, but magnificent.

"Maybe," she continued, "because I know your first choice of bedpartners last night was a bubble-headed bimbo with fake boobs. Men who lust after Feathers do not get high marks in the taste department in my book."

Oh, *Feather*. He'd forgotten about her. "You were hardly expecting to sleep solo yourself, sister," he shot back. Meanwhile, he'd managed to maneuver the brocade coverlet over far enough to grab it and wrap up a toga of his own. "Besides, you're the one who crawled in with me, not vice versa."

"You're right, I did not intend to sleep solo," she said smartly. "And you're also right that I did crawl in with you. But that was a mistake. I'm not exactly sure how it happened, but I ended up in the wrong room."

"Uh-huh. Convenient. Maybe you just picked the first door at the top of the stairs."

"For your information, I planned things rather carefully," she insisted. "Yesterday was my birthday and I was trying to arrange a very simple little fling. But did I pick some stud ten years younger than me? No! A stranger? No! I chose a decent, normal guy with an IQ well above four. Not Feather McStupid!"

"Okay, that's not funny." But he started to laugh anyway. He couldn't help it. His senses were overloading and he had to break the tension somehow. Feather McStupid? It wasn't that clever; it just hit him the right way.

"So happy to keep you entertained."

He shrugged. "I said I was sorry."

"Yeah, about four times now, like I really believe any of them." Her shoulders slumped. "I don't want to ask you for any favors, but do you have any clothes you could lend me? I have a suitcase down in my car, but I can't get down there dressed like this." Her eyes were a luminous, misty green as she gazed at him, all woebegone and miserable. "I just really need to be out of here and not talking about this anymore. This whole you-and-me-last-night thing is just too much for me."

"I'm sorry," he offered, and this time he meant it. "I have a change of clothes, for me, I mean, but nothing that would fit you. Listen, why don't I run down to your car and get your suitcase? It's the least I can do."

And it would put some very healthy distance between them.

"Well, maybe."

He swept all the way around the bed, aiming for the closet on the far wall where he'd stashed his duffel bag. "I can throw on my jeans and get down there and back really quick. Just toss me your car keys."

"Oh, no."

Her tone was so dire he stopped in his tracks. See, this was why he knew he didn't want to tangle with women like Lucie. Way too complicated. You always had to ask probing questions and pick up cues and try to be sensitive to their moods. Like it was your end of the bargain for getting to do the hokey pokey all night.

And he meant *all night*, too. Six times. He hid a smile. By all rights, he ought to be in a coma.

But Lucie made another small moan of distress, and he knew that was his cue. He turned back to her. "What?"

Her eyes wide, Lucie brandished the small plaid purse she'd been carrying last night. "My keys aren't in here. Just this." She held up a tube of lipstick. "Poisonberry Smog, Feather's trademark color."

"And this means...?"

"Our purses. We were in the ladies' room, and I accidentally hit her and then everything fell on the floor and it was a big mess and I thought this was my purse because all I saw were condoms and the room key. To 203. I thought that's what Baker said. Room 203." Still carrying the tiny bag, she sat on the edge of the bed. "So I picked up the wrong plaid bag and all of this is my fault." Her gaze lifted. "I just realized... Where do you think Feather ended up?"

"Hold on. I'm still stuck back a few minutes. You *hit* Feather? Like, a catfight in the bathroom? Is that what we're talking?" Ian shook his head. "I miss all the good stuff."

But he didn't get a chance to ponder that thought. Someone rapped hard on the outside of the door, and then his brother's voice said roughly, "Ian? You in? I need to talk to you, man. I'm desperate."

Lucie stared at him, panic in her eyes. They could hear the sound of a key grinding in the lock. His brother was coming in and there was no time to stop him.

Hell. "Kyle, don't!" he started, but all the way across the room, the latch squeaked slightly, rotating. And the door itself began to slide open.

Without thinking, they both pitched back into the bed. Lucie went headfirst, flattening herself out and pulling her sheet up over her like a shroud. Ian was right behind her, scooting down under her sheet, too, shoving her down further into the bedclothes, then flapping his own bedspread out over both of them. When he drew up his knees, he hoped there was enough disarray and confusion on the bed to camouflage Lucie from his brother's prying eyes.

By that time, Kyle was all the way into the dimly lit room, nearly at the foot of the bed. Unshaven and wild-eyed, he looked about as lousy as Ian felt. "Thank God you're here. Get up, will you? I need you."

"What the hell are you doing?" Ian demanded from his sitting position.

Jesus. Lucie was breathing on his bare hip, with her head practically in his lap. How did that happen? He slipped a hand under the covers, covering her eyes like a blindfold.

To Kyle, he growled, "I can't believe you just barged into my room at the crack of dawn. Get out of here!"

"Crack of dawn? It's after ten." Kyle strode to the window, pulling the blinds with a loud clatter that brought instant pain to Ian's head and made Lucie bounce in his lap, putting her in an even more precarious place. *Oh, man. Just don't touch anything.* He was sweating again.

"Ten o'clock?" he echoed in a strained voice. "You've got to be kidding."

"Besides, the key was in the door." Kyle peered at the mess in the room, strolling over to poke at the discarded pile of clothing. "I assumed I wasn't interrupting anything." Lifting an eyebrow, Kyle also lifted first one kilt and then the other. "Guess I was wrong. Guess you had a better night than I did."

"Guess again."

Kyle sent him a tight smile. "So you've got somebody under there, huh? Feather, maybe?" He moseyed closer to the bed, hanging a hand over the footpost. "She feeling a little shy this morning?"

"It's not Feather, and it's none of your business," Ian muttered between clenched teeth.

"So why are you hiding? You haven't got anything I didn't see in the bathtub when I was three."

"Because I thought I could protect... Oh, never mind." He leapt out the side, leaving the coverlet over Lucie and smashing the bed curtains together behind him. Still glowering at his idiot brother, Ian stalked over to the closet and rummaged around for his jeans, which was what he should've done ages ago. "You better have a pretty good explanation for this, Kyle," he said savagely, hopping into one leg and then the other. "Blasting in my door like a storm trooper, refusing to leave when it should be pretty damn clear you're intruding—"

"Look, you shouldn't have been playing pick-up on my wedding night, anyway," Kyle complained. "It's gross. And whoever she is, she's fine in there." He paused. "But it isn't Feather, right? You swear?"

"Yes, I swear. What difference does it make?"

"I need to talk to you." He dropped his voice. "About my marriage. About maybe not having a marriage. So, is it safe? To talk in front of your, uh, you know..."

"What do you want me to do, send her out into the hall naked just so you can have my undivided attention? Jeez, Kyle, you gotta be kidding." Ian pulled a T-shirt on over his head and grabbed a few things out of his bag. He headed for the bathroom not far from the closet. "Let me brush my teeth and then you and I can go to your room."

But Kyle shook his head. Hovering in the doorway to the bathroom, he announced, "I can't go back there. My new mother-in-law is up in the honeymoon suite cataloguing gifts or something."

"So we'll go down to the restaurant, have a cup of coffee while you spill your tale of woe."

"Nope." Kyle's expression grew even more bleak. "That's where I spent most of last night, sleeping on a banquette. I only left when Steffi and her father and about fifty of their friends rolled in for breakfast this morning. I didn't want to be where they were."

This sounded like one hell of a mess. Ian sighed as he splashed water on his face. "You slept on a bench in the restaurant? On your wedding night?"

Kyle wheeled away, swore, and then turned back. "You were right," he confessed. "Marrying Steffi was the biggest mistake of my life."

"I didn't think she was right for you, but I didn't think it would blow up on you this fast." Toweling off and reaching for the toothpaste, he tried, "But, hey, a lot of people fight. It doesn't mean that—"

"Yes, it does. Listen to this. She refused to sleep with me last night." Kyle shook his head. "Before we got engaged, she wanted to boogie like a bunny. Totally insatiable."

"Okay, well, keep it down, okay?" Halting his brushing, he inclined a thumb in the direction of the bed, suddenly aware this was something Lucie would not care to hear.

"Yeah, yeah. Sorry. Anyway, after we got engaged, she decided we should wait, kind of have a moratorium, make the wedding night special."

"Kind of dopey, but sounds like a woman to me." Did he hear a groan come from behind the bed curtains?

"Except that there *was* no wedding night." His brother's expression was as dark as Ian had ever seen it. "She spent the whole night opening the gifts and screaming about how much she hated everything. Screaming, at the top of her lungs, about what cheapskates people were and how they owed better presents since she spent so much on the wedding—which is a lie. Our dad threw in the Inn and all the booze and her dad owns a damn catering company. This wedding was practically free. So, anyway, I slammed out of there at like four a.m. and she was still going strong."

Ian didn't know what to say. He rinsed his mouth, finally mumbling, "Okay, that's pretty bad."

"Pretty bad? The woman is a freaking loony tune! She's selfish, she's mean, she's manipulative, she's totally immature." Kyle began to pace, his voice rising. "I didn't even tell you the worst part. You know how I said she hated all the wedding presents? Ian, she threw three toasters and a waffle iron off the balcony into the parking lot! She could've killed someone." He set his jaw in a hard line. "I only have one choice. I want a divorce."

Now there was a definite yelp from the bed. "Pssst!" he heard. Ian abandoned his toothbrush and strode to the curtains. Parting them just enough to stick his head through, he whispered, "What do you want?"

Lucie was on her hands and knees, all wrapped in the bedspread like a Christmas package. Her soft, full breasts pressed against the top fold of the brocaded fabric, and she had cleavage to spare. *Damn.* Bent over like that, her position reminded him of the time they were on the floor, naked and slippery... He closed his eyes.

"What do you think I want? He's divorcing my sister," she hissed back. "And why are your eyes closed?"

"Half sister." He forced open his eyes, but kept them focused on her face, nowhere else. "I don't see why you care. I thought you didn't like her."

"I don't! But *still*."

"Lucie, we have to talk about this later. Let me get rid of Kyle—"

"Tell him not to dump her now. The day after the wedding, it will make her furious and she will make his life hell. Tell him," she persisted. She scooted closer, twisting the bedspread around with her, keeping everything covered well enough that he could relax...for now. "I know her better than he does. Tell him he'll have to plan carefully and be very, very smart, or Steffi and my dad will take him for every dime he's got."

He noticed she didn't say that it was a rotten thing to do, to divorce her half sister about twelve hours into the marriage. No, just that Kyle needed to exercise extreme caution. That part about "every dime he's got" made an impression on Ian, all right, since he and his brother were partners in a venture that was just about to pay off big-time.

If Steffi messed up their deal...

"Who's in there and what is she saying?" Kyle demanded, yanking back the drape. "But that's... Steffi's sister? You let me tell you all this with a spy in the bed? My own brother, sleeping with the enemy?"

"I am not the enemy," Lucie protested.

Ian noticed she didn't contradict the "sleeping with" part. How could she? Except for the fact that neither of them had actually *slept*.

As she scrambled off the edge of the bed, Ian reached over and awkwardly tucked in an errant flap of her makeshift cloak. He didn't want Kyle getting any ideas.

Intent on her mission to enlighten Kyle, Lucie didn't seem to notice. "In fact," she declared, "I may be the only person who can help you. You can't just divorce Steffi. She'll have a fit."

"I don't much care," Kyle retorted.

"You'd better care," the other two said in unison.

Lucie added, "Steffi is vindictive and spoiled. And my father is deathly afraid of public embarrassment. It will become a matter of pride to both of them. You file for divorce and they will tie you and your assets up in so many knots you may never get out."

"Listen to her, Kyle," Ian interjected. "She's talking money. And your money and my money are pretty much one and the same thing."

"Yeah, but..." Kyle broke off, clearly confused. "Maybe I could annul the marriage instead."

"No, that won't be any better." Now it was Lucie's turn to pace, her bedspread whipping around her. "If only we could maneuver things so that Steffi dumped *you*..."

"Okay." Looking a bit more hopeful, Kyle inquired, "But how?"

"I don't know. Sheesh." Lucie dissolved into a heap of linen on the floor. "I feel so disloyal helping you at all, though Lord knows Steffi is reaping what she's sown for a long time. But I don't know how to pull this off. I mean, you're everything she ever wanted. Everything my dad wanted for her. All she does is brag about what a catch she's got. Money, looks, position. To her, you're like the best Ken doll ever, and you come with all kinds of good accessories, even Barbie's Dream Family. Steffi's not going to give that up without a fight."

"Barbie's what?" Kyle looked mystified. "Do you know what she's talking about?"

Ian shook his head.

"How the heck did the two of you get together, anyhow?" Kyle asked, befuddled. "I didn't even know you knew each other."

"Barely," they both said quickly.

Lucie lifted her chin. "It was an accident. We've got it all sorted out now, though. No harm, no foul. We're going to pretend it never happened, right, Ian?"

Silence hung over them for a few seconds. So she wanted to pretend it never happened. Sure, that was what he wanted, too. So why did he feel like she'd just kicked him where it counted?

"Okay, so back to Steffi dumping me..."

But Ian was at the end of his rope. His head still hurt, he needed coffee badly, and he hadn't had a chance to make things right with Lucie. Kyle would have to go.

Physically pushing his brother to the other side of the room and the exit, he announced, "Look, little brother, I appreciate that you are in a major jam. And I promise that, later, I will do my best to help you out. But right now, I have some issues of my own to work through."

Kyle dug in his heels. "What am I supposed to do? If I can't divorce her now, what do I do about the honeymoon? We're supposed to leave for Hawaii in a few hours."

"So go," Ian said sensibly. "Have a nice trip."

"I don't want to be alone with her for five minutes, let alone nine hours on a plane."

"Come on, you just married her. You had to anticipate spending some time with her," Ian argued.

"I think Kyle is right. He shouldn't go." Lucie stood there, her hands on her hips. "You're supposed to be making her sorry she married you. Going on the honeymoon is only going to make *you* sorry. Trust me on this. She'll spend all your money, she'll shop, she'll have a great time. Meanwhile, you'll be contemplating throwing yourself off a cliff."

"So what, then?" Kyle asked.

"So...think of something." She seemed to be losing her patience, and Ian didn't blame her. Besides, as he recalled last night with a twinge of pain, patience wasn't Lucie's strong suit. "Think up some reason you can't fly. You know, an illness or something."

"You could break both legs," Ian suggested.

"Wouldn't one be enough?"

"No," his brother retorted. "I've flown with people with one broken leg. But two..."

"Okay, two."

"Two broken legs? Are you guys nuts? All he needs is a sinus infection!" Lucie let out a noise that was roughly in the neighborhood of "arrrghhh" and then she muttered, "*Men.*"

"Okay, a fake sinus infection it is," Kyle put in. "So what do I do? Sniffle?"

"Sniffle and have a headache," Lucie told him. "A big headache."

"Sounds good." Ian clapped his brother on the shoulder, attempting to shepherd him through the door. But when he opened it, he heard voices and animated chatter. It sounded as if a large crowd had congregated out there.

He swung the door open the rest of the way, edging out far enough to see what the ruckus was. What the...? There were about a hundred people milling up and down the stairs outside, spilling down into the Inn's front hall. Unfortunately, they also had a full view of his door there, just off the landing where the double staircases converged.

He turned back. "What are all those people doing waiting around, staring at my door?"

"I don't know," Kyle said with a shrug. "Steffi's going to come down the stairs so everybody can clap or something. I'm supposed to stand at the bottom and wait for her. And then they all throw rice and we take off in our limo."

"Ian?" his mother's voice called from somewhere on the staircase. "Is Kyle with you?"

Ian stepped out to the top of the big double staircase, where he felt like he was holding court. "Mom, Kyle's not feeling well. But he'll be right out to tell you himself." Over his shoulder, he remarked, "Time to be a man, Kyle. Remember, sniffles and headache."

"Yeah, yeah." But he did it, trudging down the stairs like he was going to his execution.

"Kyle, you look terrible!" about five people chorused. That ought to make the sinus infection ruse go over better.

Breathing a sigh of relief, Ian went back to room 203, removed the key, slid into his room, and securely closed the door behind him with a reassuring snap.

"Okay," he said, folding his arms over his T-shirt. "Now we decide what to do about you and me."

"What's to decide?" Lucie was busy buttoning on his shirt from last night over her underwear. If he had to guess, he would say she was taking the tactic that if she ignored it, it would go away. "Oh, your shirt had buttons so I borrowed it. I hope you don't mind. It's not great, but it covers the important bits, and it should get me down to my car. It's a Jeep—you know, the kind with the canvas windows?—so I should be able to slash my way in with a pocketknife. You don't have one, do you? No biggie. Do you happen to know how to hot-wire a car? I think I know, in theory, but I could use some help."

He laughed out loud at how matter-of-fact she made it sound. "Do you know how many people are standing outside our door? And you think you're going to waltz through all of them, barefoot, wearing a man's shirt and no bottoms, and calmly break into your car and then hot-wire it?"

She threw up her hands. "I apparently lost my granny boots at some point before I got here last night, and my bridesmaid outfit doesn't have any fasteners. What else am I supposed to do?"

"Well, for one thing, I can go try to find Feather and your keys, and then get your suitcase. Or I can borrow some clothes from my mother or my sister. It's the least I can do." He knew his smile was smug, but she was being so silly. "It's a lot smarter than trying to run the gauntlet."

As he spoke, Lucie looked madder and madder, practically wringing her hands with dismay. "Look." Her lips were all tight and she wouldn't meet his eyes. "It should be perfectly obvious to both of us by now that this was just some big, unexpected joke of fate and we are not at all *anything* to each other. Agreed?"

He nodded reluctantly.

"Right. So you don't have to be nice to me or gallant or any of that kind of nonsense." She started to make choppy, flustered gestures with her hands, as her words tumbled over each other, faster and faster. "In case you haven't noticed, I am incredibly embarrassed and upset and...I don't know what! I don't even know what happened, and I don't want to know, although I'm scared to death I'm going to remember. But in the meantime, before I do remember and feel the need to slash my wrists, the sooner I'm out of here and we get on our way to never seeing each other again as long as we live, the better."

She let out a big breath. He was still stunned from the torrent she'd just let loose, and he didn't even open his mouth. Too late now. She had started again.

"And if you say, 'It's the least I can do' to me one more time, I swear I will strangle you with my bare hands!"

"But you don't have to be embarrassed. I'm not." He protested, blocking her way as she attempted to circle around him.

"Of course you're not. You sleep around all the time. *I* don't!" she retorted.

"I'm actually insulted you think that."

She reached for the doorknob. "All I meant is that you're probably more used to this kind of awkward morning-after stuff than I am."

"Not like this," he grumbled under his breath. "Lucie, please, just give me a chance—"

"To what? Remind me of what a very bizarre and stupid thing I did?" She shook her head, prying his hand off the door. "I have to go, Ian. I'm sorry I screwed up your fling with Feather but I have a feeling she'll be available again if you really want to hook up with her."

He stepped to the side, allowing her enough room to leave if she was determined to go. Given the crowd outside and her bedraggled outfit, she was almost certainly going to regret running out there, but he could hardly physically stop her. "I meant to thank you for hijacking my key from Feather, even if it was an acci-

dent. I think I definitely got the better part of that
exchange and I'd much rather be sharing this awkward
morning with you than her."

"There you go," she murmured, "being gallant
again." This time she looked him in the eye. "I really
hate that."

4

LUCIE TOOK a deep breath, opened the door, and took about a step and a half into the real world. She stopped in her tracks.

"Oh, no," she whispered. "This is terrible."

Self-conscious, she smoothed her hair away from her face. Not that it was going to help anything.

Ian had warned her that there were all kinds of people outside his room. But not this many. Not all dressed up and fresh faced and curious, staring up at the top of the stairs, right where she was rooted to the carpet, wearing a man's rumpled shirt and no shoes. They had expectation on their faces and little bundles of rice in their hands.

And Steffi. *No, please no.* Not Steffi, too.

But there she was, wearing a pretty lavender suit and a corsage, with her mother and their mutual father right behind her. All three of them were poised on the landing, only a few yards from Lucie and the door to room 203.

They turned, all three of them. They saw her. Their faces reflected first shock and then outrage. Steffi reacted first. And Lucie would've bet you could hear the scream emanating from her sister's throat from down in the front hall all the way up to the top turret on the

Highland Inn. Just in case there was one man, woman or child *not* staring at Lucie's disgrace.

"Do you see that?" Steffi shrieked. "Lucie, sneaking out of some man's room wearing nothing but his shirt. Just look at her!"

There were shushing sounds, but it was too late. The damage was done.

"What are you doing?" Steffi cried, stalking closer and raking Lucie with her furious glare. "Look at you, barely managing to crawl out of some stranger's bed on the morning after my wedding. *My* wedding!" As Donald Webster moved behind her to support her, she turned into his shoulder, sobbing, "Oh, Daddy, what else can happen? First it rained and then the hem of my dress got wet and then someone sneezed during the ceremony and some loser gave my maid of honor a black eye—"

"A black eye? Really?" Huh. She didn't think she'd hit Feather that hard.

But Steffi was on a roll and not brooking interruptions. "And then the presents were cheap and tacky and Kyle got a cold or something and now *this*. My entire wedding is *ruined*. Oh, Daddy, how could she?"

"I don't know, sweetie," he said gruffly, patting her ineffectually. His face was red and puffed up with anger, but at least he kept his voice down when he demanded, "Lucie, what do you have to say for yourself?"

"Not a heck of a lot," she murmured. "I'm really sorry that this happened, but—"

"She's trying to humiliate me in front of my new in-laws, Daddy."

"No, she isn't." It was Ian, sounding much sterner than she'd ever heard him as he stepped out behind her, his duffel bag looped over one shoulder. She tried to stop him, but he was already saying, "Lucie was with me."

"What?" If Steffi's previous shriek had been high on the decibel scale, this one was off the charts.

Lucie winced. The spoiled princess finding out her half sister had picked up a man at her wedding was one thing. In fact, Steffi might've actually enjoyed that part, what with all the drama and the chance to be right in the center of a soap opera and suck up sympathy.

But now that Steffi knew Lucie had not just picked up any man, but had slept with a carbon copy of her groom…? Oooh, this was going to get ugly. Steffi never had liked sharing her toys. And Lucie felt very sure that was how her half sister viewed the whole charmed Mackintosh family—as if she got to slap "property of Steffi" stickers on their hands and feet, just like every doll she'd ever owned.

Now, Steffi's eyes narrowed to slits. "You always have to find some way to wreck things for me, don't you?"

"Well, no—" Lucie started, thinking that Steffi did a pretty good job of that on her own, but she didn't get very far.

"Lucie, this is disgusting, even for you," Ginetta interrupted, sticking her thin nose in the air. "Pushing yourself on the Mackintoshes, taking advantage of someone as kind as Ian, and then parading around like a tramp in front of all of us just to steal attention on your sister's wedding day. How could you?"

"The wedding was yesterday," Lucie pointed out quietly.

"Does it matter?" demanded Ginetta.

Ian leaned close to her ear. "I can't believe you're letting them talk to you like this."

"I'm sort of used to it."

"That's no excuse."

"What are you two whispering about?" Steffi interrupted. "Is she trying to poison you against me, Ian? For Kyle's sake, don't let her do that."

"Kyle doesn't tell me who to be with, and I don't tell him, either," Ian said coldly. He set a strong arm around Lucie's shoulders, steering her around the Webster family roadblock and toward the stairs. "Look, here's the deal. Lucie and I are what you might call an item."

"Ian, you don't have to—"

But he cut her off. "It's the least I can do," he said with a mischievous wink, firmly guiding her down the first few steps. "We've been together, oh, for a while now. But, hey, we didn't want to steal Steffi and Kyle's thunder, so we kept it quiet and tried to keep our hands off each other in public, out of respect...yadda yadda yadda. You know the drill."

"I don't believe it for a minute," Steffi scoffed.

"Believe it." It was wrong, but Lucie couldn't help herself. She stopped, turned back, and smiled at Steffi. Smiled. *Ha! Take that!* "We were only thinking of you,

Steffi. I knew how you would feel about us getting together so close to your wedding, so I convinced Ian our relationship should be a secret. But we're crazy about each other and, last night, we both had a little too much to drink, and—"

"And we couldn't deny it any longer," Ian finished, backing her up. "So we stayed together in my room—"

"Because we couldn't stay in my room, which was halfway to Wisconsin," Lucie added sweetly.

"Right." When he glanced down at her, she saw a definite sparkle of amusement in his beautiful blue eyes. "But we didn't plan ahead and Lucie didn't bring any clothes. Our mistake. It was the heat of passion. What can you say?"

"That's about it." Lucie stood there in the middle of the staircase, enjoying the enraged expression on her half sister's face. She also felt some guilt, but she did her best to squash it. Steffi deserved it. "Any questions?"

"This isn't finished, Lucie. Not by a long shot," her father bristled. She'd been expecting him to get in his licks.

Now he would undoubtedly bring up her inheritance from her mother, the company he was supposedly holding onto until she proved she was mature enough to handle it. He always threw that in her face when things got complicated. Lucie pressed her lips together, waiting for the inevitable.

He didn't disappoint her. "You want me to treat you like an adult and yet you behave like this, doing your best to ruin this important day for Steffi. You may never get the company at this rate."

"I wasn't holding my breath, Dad."

"Lucie?" Ian nudged her down the steps. "We should probably get moving."

Poor Ian. He was undoubtedly embarrassed beyond belief at this unpleasant commotion. Lucie ducked her head and let him lead the way. They were almost at the bottom when the other side of the family chimed in.

"Ian?" *Uh-oh.* It was his mother, the lovely and gracious Myra Mackintosh, waiting patiently near the door. "What is this all about?"

Ian hesitated, and Lucie sped up so she could explain things first. She owed him. Scrambling down the steps, she said earnestly, "Mrs. Mackintosh, I'm so sorry. It's not what it looks like. Well, actually, it is kind of what it looks like, but it was just a mistake and—"

"Now, really, dear, I think it's Ian who should be apologizing, don't you?" his mother said dryly.

"No, not really—"

"Sorry, Mom," he offered automatically.

"I'll just bet you are. All right, darling, get the poor thing out of here, why don't you? At least find her some shoes. We'll speak about this later." She stepped back, clearing a path to the Inn's massive front door, held open by a man in—what else?—a kilt. "Nice to meet you, dear," she called after them.

Safely out the door, Lucie glanced up at Ian. "'Nice to meet you'? 'At least find her some shoes'?" She laughed. "Your mother was so calm. Does this happen often to you? Is your mother used to catching barefoot women sneaking out of your bedroom after a night of wild passion?''

"Not often, no," he returned, lowering his voice and gesturing that she should do the same.

Looking around, she understood why he wanted to keep it down. There were wedding guests out here under the portico, too, plus clumps of them standing with umbrellas under the cloudy June sky, holding rice, ready to toss. Lucie tried to paste on a smile, but they still regarded her as if she had "harlot" stenciled on her forehead.

What did she expect? They'd just heard her talking about wild passion and sneaking out of Ian's bedroom. And they could see for themselves what a mess she was with her strange attire and bare feet and unkempt hair.

"Carry on," she said loudly, waving at them. A well-dressed matron sniffed and another woman hid her daughter's eyes.

Lucie slunk around the corner toward the parking lot. Could things get any worse?

Ian had tried to warn her it wouldn't be so easy to just stroll out of the Highland Inn, and she hadn't listened. Well, now she was sorry.

"You know," she said out loud. "My dad's been telling me for years that I'm an irresponsible twit who hasn't got a clue how to run my life. I guess it was time I finally proved him right."

Looking way too gorgeous for someone as sweet as he was behaving, Ian bent down and ruffled her hair. She hated that, especially from him. It made her feel about six years old. On the other hand, it also made her feel as if last night had never happened. *Could* never have happened.

"Lucie, you are way too hard on yourself," he said gently, following her onto the paved parking lot. "None of those people know you. And they'll never remember."

"They know *you*. They're going to be greeting you for years going, 'Who was that crazy woman in your shirt at your brother's wedding? What was that all about?'" Lucie let out an aggrieved sigh. "I'm afraid you're going to bear the brunt of this one."

"It's as much my fault as yours. So I guess I deserve it."

"Nice try." She gave him a sly smile. "But, hey, good save there at the top of the stairs. That was terrific. You'll probably never live it down and your mother is going to blister your hide, but it was very gallant. Again."

"It was the least I could do."

Lucie laughed, running ahead of him as it started to sprinkle. "I really am going to have to kill you. You know that, don't you?"

But her laughter died when she spotted her Jeep. Unless her eyes were playing tricks on her—entirely possible, given her state of stress and exhaustion—the top had caved in. Racing to it, climbing up on the sideboard, paying no attention to the fact that the rain was coming down harder now, she saw that something had hurtled down from the sky, slashing a deep gash in the canvas top of her car and smashing the windshield to smithereens. A waffle iron. A waffle iron from the sky. The shiny appliance was sitting in the middle of the dashboard. Or half of it, anyway.

Meanwhile, a toaster had dented the car next to hers, plus another toaster and some shards of china lay broken on the pavement. Toasters, waffle irons and china falling from the sky? All she could do was gape up into the rain, gazing at the balcony jutting out from the fourth floor above her head.

"Steffi strikes again," Ian murmured, opening up a small umbrella he'd pulled from the side of his duffel bag. "Your Jeep was parked under the honeymoon suite. On the bright side, you won't need to break in to get your suitcase."

As Lucie lingered by the car, speechless, he reached in through the wreckage and pulled a tapestry overnight bag from the back seat. He waited there, carrying her suitcase, holding his umbrella at the ready. "Lucie, can I offer you a ride home?"

She didn't want to impose on Ian any more this morning. But what choice did she have?

Swearing under her breath, Lucie still hung onto the door of her beloved Jeep, getting wetter and wetter in the downpour. She had no shoes, no keys, no car, no reputation... And all because of one stupid fling. Other people flung all the time and nobody was the wiser. She did it once and her life went to hell in a handbasket.

"Ian, if the offer for the ride still stands..." She hopped off the sideboard. "I'd love to."

SHE HAD TO admit it—Ian Mackintosh was excellent company, and very handy to have around. Damn him, anyway.

He had a big, comfortable sedan, he had paper towels to blot off some of the rain—he even had a supply of granola bars and bottled water. Drinking greedily, Lucie settled into the passenger seat, gazing out the tinted window and wishing she could go back about twenty-four hours and try again.

But if she had to have a disastrous fling, she supposed Ian was the person to do it with. She spared him a quick glance. Not only was he incredibly cute, but he'd stood up for her and then offered her a ride home. What more could you ask?

She shifted awkwardly in her seat. Maybe someone not quite so athletic in bed would've been better. She still didn't have a firm grasp on the details—thank heavens—but her body was sore enough in strange enough places that she knew it had to have been steamier than anything in her imagination.

And now, here she was, stuck in a car with him. Every mile that they traveled was one mile closer to her modest, private place, her sanctuary. Her house. Flings were supposed to be nameless and faceless, weren't they? They weren't supposed to turn your life upside down, drive up to your front door, and invade your personal boundaries.

Lucie couldn't think of one man she'd dated who'd set foot in her house. That was mostly her fault, because she didn't keep things very neat and she always had underwear lying around everywhere. But *still*...

She hazarded another glance Ian's way. Was she obligated to ask him in? What was the etiquette after you'd explored every inch of each other's bodies? This was way beyond her experience.

She sat there, stewing. How had everything gone so wrong in such a short time?

Okay, time to perk up. So what if she now had this bizarre, instantly intimate relationship with a stranger? So what if her entire family hated her? So what if now, after this debacle, her father never would turn over Pandora's Boxers, the company that should've been hers years ago?

"Damn it, anyway. I was *this* close," she whispered. "I know I could've talked him into it. But not now."

Oh, pooh. Who was she kidding? Her father had no intention of giving her Pandora's Boxers, no matter what she did.

"What did you say? Something about socks?" Ian asked. He turned down the volume on the radio.

"Socks. I need to put on some socks." Leaving her dashed dreams about Pandora's Boxers for later, she turned her focus to more practical matters, squeezing through the opening to the back seat to drag her suitcase closer. After rooting around, she found socks, shoes and a pair of pajama pants she could pull on right there in the passenger seat.

"If we're in a wreck, you're good to go," he offered, checking on her progress.

Lucie bent over her bag, groping for a hairbrush and a scrunchie. "You planning to be in a wreck?"

"Nope." He raised an eyebrow. "You?"

"I hope not. But the way my luck's been running today, I wouldn't bet against one. Keep your eyes on the road, okay?" She pulled down the visor, got one glimpse of her too-pale face and the wild state of her hair, and slammed it back up. She found a couple of pencils in her bag, wound her hair into a lump, and secured it with the pencils. "I look like the wreck of the Hesperus."

"What's that?"

"I don't know. Something my mom always used to say." Lucie shrugged, wishing she hadn't mentioned it. It was probably because she'd been thinking about Pandora's Boxers, her mother's old company. But the last thing she wanted was to share misty memories with Ian, her one and only one-night stand.

"Are you close to your mother?"

She knew he was just making conversation, and she could've just said no. But she wasn't going to lie to him. "My mother died when I was twelve."

"I'm sorry." Ian's expression was rueful. "I think I've said that more today than in the rest of my life combined."

Lucie smiled. "So maybe you'd better stop apologizing."

"Maybe. I guess that means you grew up with Don and Steffi and what's-her-name, the Wicked Witch?" He shook his dark head. "That bites."

"Not really." She lifted her shoulders in a careless shrug. "I mean, not really, I didn't grow up with them. I kind of lived on the outskirts—part of the time with my aunt and part with my dad and Ginetta, except not

with them. You'll see when we get to my place. I still
live on the outskirts. But it's also not really something I
want to talk about, so..." Forcefully, she changed the
subject. "So, Ian, what do you do? I mean, as a job. Do
you work for your dad with the golf course thing?"

It seemed really strange asking him basic questions
like that. Everything was so mixed up. *Where did you
get that cute little scar below your belly button and oh, by the
way, what do you do for a living?* But he didn't seem to
notice.

"I used to work for my dad's company. But then
Kyle and I set up a business of our own. And we're
cashing in." He grinned. "So pretty soon I won't be doing anything."

"I don't understand. Cashing in?"

He shrugged. "It's really boring. We created this Internet thing. We're in the process of selling it to someone else who is willing to pay us a lot for it. That's
about it."

"An Internet thing?" That was not what she
would've guessed. *Oh, I sail the Seven Seas, swashbuck-
ling by day, and then I'm a secret crime-fighter and professional basketball player by night.* "How did you get
started in that?"

"By accident." With his hand looped over the steering wheel, Ian yawned, reminding her that neither of
them had gotten much sleep last night. Lucie stifled
her own yawn, resting her head on the back of the seat
and sipping from her water bottle as he continued.
"Kyle and I both used to work for Dad's company, de-
veloping golf resorts. It was fine, but we were getting

bored. So we started playing around on our own time and we got this brilliant idea to do this virtual tour of golf courses around Chicago. It's pretty cool, actually. Only then we wanted to know who was playing our virtual golf courses, so we sort of invented this marketing info collection system..." He sent her a quick look. "Boring, huh?"

"No, not at all," she hurried to assure him. "I just don't know anything about that stuff. I'm actually starting to—it's one of my summer projects—but for right now, I'm still kind of technologically impaired."

"Me, too. But we got lucky. Or we will when the deal goes through." He lifted his shoulders. "It should be quite a lot of cash. And this isn't my dad's money, or his dad's. This is our own windfall, Kyle's and mine—unless Steffi gets in the way." His expression darkened.

All Lucie could think of was that Ian Mackintosh was even more of a catch than she'd first thought. If you were into that. Which she wasn't.

But there was no denying the facts—Ian was gorgeous, sexier than hell, kind enough to rescue disheveled damsels in distress, and backed up by a wonderful family. On top of that, he was wealthy in his own right, and unlike other successful men she knew, this one wouldn't be spending every waking minute on his job because he was retiring at the grand old age of...what? Thirty? Thirty-five?

She didn't even know how old he was. Once again, she was struck by how stupid it was to go flinging with a stranger. "How old are you?"

He blinked. "Thirty-two. Why? How old are you?"

"I just turned thirty. Yesterday, as a matter of fact."

"Oh. So, uh, with me, last night, was that your way of throwing yourself a party?"

Some party. "I guess you could look at it that way."

A long pause hung between them.

It didn't escape her that half the women in Chicago would die to change places with her, riding around with Mr. Eligible Bachelor. And all she wanted was to go home and take a nap and pretend he didn't exist.

After that depressing little exchange, what with her orphan status and her calamitous thirtieth birthday, she could see him mentally changing gears, trying to lighten the mood in here. "So how about you, Lucie? What do you do for a living?"

"Oh, well, now *that's* boring. I teach at a private school for girls." She gazed out at the green countryside passing her window. Not so far from home now. Not far from bringing Ian into her inner sanctum. *No, Lucie, he's already been there. And then some.* She shook her head to clear those horrifying thoughts, but the images remained. Ian, buck naked, sliding off the bed. Ian, ragingly aroused, sliding into her...

She choked, sitting up straighter and gulping down water from her bottle. She was trying to block all that out. If only the bits and pieces in her disjointed memory would cooperate.

"Are you okay?"

"No, but I will be," she mumbled. *When you leave and my life goes back to normal and I'm plain old Lucie the Nitwit again instead of Lucie the Harlot.*

"Okay, so you're a teacher. What subject?"

"Sort of a hodgepodge. I do arts and crafts, sewing, stagecraft, even a little woodworking. In my classes, we make birdhouses and decoupage, Halloween costumes and papier-mâché masks." She'd explained this one a million times and she used her familiar refrain. "If you can make it with your hands, I can teach you how."

"Well, that's different."

Poor Ian. He was really working to keep this lame conversation going so that neither of them would have time to think about all the other things they were really thinking about.

"It's not much, but it's respectable," Lucie said in the most annoyingly cheery voice she could come up with. "It's enough to pay the rent and keep my dad off my back. At least until this weekend's fiasco. Oh, wait." She leaned into her window, relieved beyond belief to see the gates of home. "My turn's coming up. Right here, between the brick pillars."

He peered through the rain-spattered windshield, no doubt gaping at the squatty brick mansion that sat like a big fat toad at the end of the long circular drive. Mushroom brown, it had green shutters and awnings scattered willy-nilly, wherever someone had felt like adding an overhang or tacking on a few more windows.

Ian inquired politely, "Is this your father's house?" Since he could very well have said, *Bleah! That place is hideous*, Lucie appreciated his tact.

"The big house is his. I live around back." She

pointed to a small gravel lane winding off to one side. "Down there. I live in the carriage house. Well, they call it the carriage house. It looks more like a cottage. Besides, it was built way after carriages went the way of the dodo bird."

"You know, you talk a lot."

"I've been told that." Why was she so nervous? What could he do? He'd probably just drop her at the door, glad to be rid of her, and all this mental turmoil would be for nothing.

"So this is where you live," he said, grabbing her bag, sprinting out of the rain to the doorway of the small, snug story-and-a-half cottage. "I like it much better than your dad's house back there."

"Me, too."

It appeared Ian was not planning to drop her and run.

After kneeling to retrieve the spare key from under a flowerpot, Lucie had no choice but to lead the way inside, into the modest living room. It wasn't too sloppy, thank goodness. As he stood there expectantly, she shoved aside some magazines and newspapers on an overstuffed ottoman to clear a spot for him to sit—temporarily.

"So." She chewed her lip, making a move toward the stairs, trying to send him a message. "I would really like to, oh, I don't know, take a bath and then a nap. I'm kind of sleep deprived, you know." He opened his mouth and she rushed in with a fake laugh and, "But of course, you *know*. You were there."

"Yeah, I was." Ian wasn't smiling.

Uh-oh. Here it came. He was going to say he was sorry for last night—again—and she would have to say, *No, really, it was nothing. I had a good time, didn't you?* when good time didn't begin to describe it. And once he was sure he was forgiven and there were no hard feelings, then he would, oh, kiss her on the cheek or something and that would be that. And then surely he would leave and she would never see him again.

Whew. Not so horrible. Nothing she couldn't handle.

She steeled herself, ready for the big exit. But he didn't make it. Instead, he leaned forward, clasping his hands together, and announced thoughtfully, "I've been thinking."

Lucie paused. "About...?"

"About you."

"Well, okay, it's a free country and you can do that if you want to, but I don't think it's going to get you very far." She scrambled over to the other side of the living room, busying herself arranging volumes on a bookshelf.

"I don't know what you're doing over there, but you don't have to," Ian said tersely. "I'm not going to bite you."

Yeah, but did you last night? You did, didn't you? You bit me, you licked me, I bit you, I licked... And, God, this wasn't helping, was it?

"Lucie, what I meant was..." He started over. "When I told you that Kyle and I were cashing in our company very soon, it made me think. About Kyle and Steffi and how much trouble she could cause us."

"Really?" This was out of left field. Here she'd imagined he was agonizing over the flotsam and jetsam from last night's shipwreck, like she was, but all he was thinking about was his brother.

"You told Kyle that you know Steffi better than any of us," he began, "that you might be his only hope—to get out from under the marriage, I mean."

"I don't think I can—"

"But we might be able to come up with something, some plan, if we put our heads together."

"Our heads? Together?"

He smiled. She was a goner.

His expression was logical and sensible, and his classic features were so adorable, so appealing, the way his narrow lips curved into a perfect bow there in the middle, the way his blue, blue eyes lit up when he was being sincere.

She found a backbone, or at least a way to weasel out of this terrifying situation. "I can't think about this now. I need you to leave."

"I know you're exhausted. I am, too." His tone grew even more winning. "So here's what I think. We could both use a bath and a nap. You're home, but I'm a good hour and a half from my house. So, to save time, we could both clean up and catch our naps here. What do you think? An hour? Two? And then we'll come back to the subject refreshed and ready to come up with the perfect way to extract Kyle."

Extracting Kyle wasn't high on her list of priorities. Extracting herself was. Lucie beat a path to the door, which she opened for him. "That would be nice, except for the fact that you're going to leave now and never come back."

But Ian stayed where he was on her favorite over-stuffed ottoman. "If I leave, you won't have a way back to pick up your car."

"My car isn't driveable, anyway. If you leave, I will call a tow truck."

"Fair enough." He seemed to be daring her. "But why should I leave?"

"You know very well why!" She was hot and tired and she was wearing his shirt. It smelled like him. *She* smelled like him. She was simply unable to reason under these circumstances. "Because you and I... Well, I... Because we *flung*. Together. And we need to put that behind us just as soon as we can. And we can't—I can't—if I have to look at you."

"It was just a little fling. You said it yourself. No harm, no foul."

"Okay, but I was being ridiculous when I said that."

He didn't move. Rather than stand there with the door open, she shut it neatly and then slid down the inside of it until she was slumped on the floor. *I am not a person who crumbles like this.* But he was being such a jerk, talking about his brother, when she wanted him to... What *did* she want him to do? She had no idea.

Good grief, this was all so confusing.

Over there on her ottoman, she heard Ian swear, something fierce and low. She also heard his footsteps as he ambled over and joined her by the door. And then she could sense him, hovering there.

"Lucie, I know you're upset and I'm sorry—"

"You said you were going to stop saying that."

"I lied."

"I know. You have a habit of doing that, don't you?"

He swore again, louder this time. "You want to help Kyle or not?"

"Yes. No. I suppose. I don't really care."

"He's a great guy, Lucie," he said softly. "He deserves better than being shackled to your sister."

She lifted her head. "Half sister."

"Like I didn't see that coming." Ian shoved his hands in the pockets of his jeans. "Okay, so you don't care about my brother or me or the fact that Steffi stands to take a big chunk out of my Internet deal when she doesn't deserve a penny. But how about the way she treats you? She's clearly been a thorn in your side for a good, long time. Are you ready for payback?"

Okay, so that was more persuasive. "Maybe."

"Good." Now he knelt down, his head only inches from hers. "You know Steffi. And I know you'll be able to think of some way to convince her she's the one who wants out of that marriage, something good enough to make her want it quick and painless."

"I don't know... I just can't think of any way I can help you. And I don't understand why this has to be *now*." She began to say once again that she simply couldn't think right now, but instead went with, "What's wrong with tomorrow or the next day?"

"Money," he answered succinctly. "I don't know how long it's going to take for our Internet deal to go through. It should've been cleared by now. I can try to stall it for a few days, but if I can't, if the checks are in the mail, Steffi will never let him go. Besides, Kyle isn't the most devious guy in the world. That sinus infection won't last long."

"Okay, but I can't promise—"

"I know, I know. You need a bath and a nap. It won't hurt me, either." He stood up, offering her a hand. "We can clean up, lie down for a few minutes—I'll be happy to take the couch. When we wake up, we can pretend we're starting this day over. We'll both feel a lot better."

"It doesn't sound so bad," she admitted. As long as she got into the bathtub in the next five minutes, she figured she would agree to anything. "But you should know that I don't think I'm going to change my mind. I don't expect to come up with any master plan in the next few hours."

He nodded. "Fair enough."

At that, Lucie rose, neatly sidestepping him and his outstretched hand. "You won't need the couch—I have a guest room, right down the hall, second door on the left. Your bathroom is across from it. Meanwhile, I'm going upstairs to my room, and I plan to take a really long bath, so don't expect me down anytime soon."

When she reached the top of the stairs, she could see he had already started down the hall, out of sight.

So she stripped out of his damn shirt and tossed it over the side of the stairwell, back down into the living room. "Good riddance," she muttered. If she never saw—or smelled—that particular piece of cloth again as long as she lived, it would be too soon.

The shirt wafted down to the first floor like a white
flag.

"Don't even think it," she told herself out loud. "You
are not surrendering anything to Ian Mackintosh."

Not in this lifetime.

5

IAN TURNED his face full into the shower spray, relishing the feel of the cool water sluicing down his body, washing his fatigue away. He couldn't believe it, but he was actually smiling.

How did that happen? His brother was trapped in a marriage with an idiot, they stood to lose millions of dollars if he couldn't extract said brother without a costly divorce, half his parents' friends undoubtedly thought he was a sleazebucket after this morning's performance, *and* he was showering in the home of a woman who probably hated him.

And he was happy?

Go figure. Maybe he was still drunk from last night. But he didn't think so. Nah, he thought this had more to do with Lucie. There was just something about her.

And it wasn't the sex, although that had pretty much blown him away. God, he'd love to get his hands on her when he was completely sober and try all those tricks over again...and again...

His smile widened. Who'd ever have looked at unassuming, somewhat flaky Lucie and immediately thought of sizzling, steamy sex?

Well, he did *now*.

Not that he was interested in Lucie in any kind of

dating thing—she was *so* not his type—but he might be interested in getting her back in the bedroom. More to the point, he was just beginning to put together a plan whereby they could really help each other out. No details yet, no firm idea, but his mind was percolating.

He hadn't had this much fun since the early days when he and Kyle spent hours fooling around with their first virtual golf course. Yep, there was just something intriguing going on here. Something he couldn't resist.

So she was a little shy about the night they'd shared. She'd get over it.

Still grinning, Ian finished up his shower and toweled off. After a quick peek out the door to make sure the hallway was still empty, he picked up the bundle of his clothes and headed for the spare bedroom she'd pointed out.

But he was no more than a foot in the door when he lost his grin. In fact, his jaw dropped.

It wasn't that unusual a room—a double bed with a quilt tossed on it, a plain oak dresser, a couple of folding chairs—but it was covered with underwear. Men's underwear. Although there were a few pairs of pajama bottoms and a smattering of boxer shorts, most of them were briefs and whatever you called those half-and-half kind, like briefs only with longer legs. Boxerbriefs, he thought vaguely.

And they weren't the plain white or gray cotton ones, either. No, these were a riot of vivid colors, wild patterns and bizarre fabrics, everything from a pair of stretchy black velvet bikini briefs at the foot of the bed to candy-striped, sharply contoured boxers tossed on the chair nearest the door.

"What the...?"

Whose was all this stuff? And who'd left it scattered around like the backstage dressing room at Chippendales?

Ian was astonished. He'd never seen anything like it. Part of him hesitated to touch anything, but the display was too weird to ignore. Gingerly, he lifted a pair of slinky zebra-striped briefs, barely fingering the fine fabric, noticing the unusually large pouch in the front.

He dropped them like the plague.

But Ian was getting more curious by the moment. Who the hell did these things belong to? He snatched up a glow-in-the-dark, green jungle-print pair, unable to miss the fact that these, too, had a front compartment big enough for Paul Bunyan. And so did the zebra bikini briefs and the red stretch velvet boxer-briefs and even the plain navy briefs. His mistake. They weren't plain. They had a yellow moon appliquéd on the butt and a sun on the crotch. A *big* sun to go over that monstrous fly.

He'd never known any guy in any locker room in America who wore anything like these fabrics or colors or needed anything like the oversize pouches.

What, was she sleeping with a porn star? And if so, where *was* the porn star?

Why would he have left all his crazy underwear at Lucie's house, in her guest room? Who was this mythical, overendowed porn star, anyway?

Ian stalked to the closet, but it was bare except for a

few hangers. The drawers in the dresser were similarly empty. No clues there, except that the porn star apparently didn't bother with clothes, just undies.

But he still didn't get it. If Lucie had a boyfriend, why didn't she bring him to the wedding? If it was just a sex thing, if she was embarrassed by her superstud and didn't bring him out in public, then she still should logically have been running home to him for more fun and games instead of looking for flings at her half sister's wedding.

Okay, he was really getting ticked now. Grabbing up four or five of the offending garments, he stomped out in the hall, realized he wasn't wearing anything but a towel, stomped back into the guest room, found his jeans and jammed himself in, zipped up, retrieved the pile of proof, and stomped back out and up the stairs before he had a chance to think better of it.

At the top of the stairs, he stopped. He saw three doors. One was partially open, and it led to a light, airy bedroom, all yellow and white, with a wicker bed and rocker. Very pretty. But no blizzard of outrageous undies. And no Lucie.

The second door was a closet. And the third... He could hear music behind door number three. Ian yanked it open, brandishing underwear like a sword.

There she was all right, asleep in a big, claw-footed white tub, her head resting on a small pillow, her arms propped on the sides. She'd pulled her hair into a haphazard topknot, with wet, silky tendrils spilling down at her temples and the nape of her neck. A boombox sat on the floor, a woman's voice singing about love and longing. Sarah McLachlan, maybe.

When he came crashing in, Lucie awoke, but not completely. "Huh?" She sat up, her eyes unfocused but gradually clearing. "Ian? Is there an emergency?"

As she became more alert, she also seemed to notice that her bubbles were fading and his gaze was fixed on the mounds of her luscious breasts, floating there half in and half out of the water. He could see the dark look she sent him before she slid down farther, until only her head and knees were visible.

"This better be good," was all she said.

Meanwhile, he was trying to regain the momentum of his anger. For a minute there, he was distracted enough by wet, supple skin, easing in and out of view with every breath, that his mission hadn't seemed very important. But as his gaze skimmed the underwear still clasped in his hand, he was irate all over again. Just the thought of Lucie and her slender curves crushed under some colossus...

"Whose are these?" he demanded, holding up the rainbow of briefs and boxers.

She glanced over, frowned, and looked away. She had that stubborn tilt back to her chin. "What business is it of yours?"

"I'd like to be prepared," he said angrily, "in case the guy who fits in these things comes storming in and tries to take my head off for sleeping in his bed."

"I should've guessed. Macho stuff." She closed her eyes and hummed along with her boombox for a few bars, but her jaw was clenched tight. "Okay, well, if that's all you're worried about, I can promise no one is going to come storming in looking for his underpants, okay? Good enough?"

"No." He flapped them in his fist. "I want to know who these belong to. Porn star? Chippendales dancer? Anybody else who pads his pants with a stuffed sock?"

"Oh, please."

He waited, scowling at the briefs.

"Me," Lucie said finally. "They belong to me. And I need you to put them back, because I had them laid out in the order I want them worn."

"What? Just what kind of kinky business do you have going on in this house?" He'd gone from annoyance to outrage in a few seconds. Maybe it was just because he'd misjudged her so badly. He'd actually thought she was *shy*. "What are you, cracking a whip over some weird submissive superstud, making him model triple-X underpants for you?"

She sat up, her eyes wide and her mouth gaping. "It's not kinky. It's lingerie. It's... If you must know, those are Pandora's Boxers."

"Who the hell is Pandora?" Some cross-dressing freakazoid friend who stayed over in Lucie's guest room?

"Pandora *was* my mother." With a prim snort of disapproval, Lucie leaned over the edge and snagged a towel. She stood up, neatly wrapping herself in the towel, as coy as a stripper with a giant fan, and then fixed him with a very snippy smile. "This is going to take a while—the explanation, I mean. So you might as well take my boxers—well, those are mostly brixers, actually—get out of my bathroom before I find something lethal to throw at you, go back downstairs and wait for me. Which is what I told you to do in the first place, if you recall."

There was a lot there to chew on, not the least of which was "brixers." Her mother? What would her mother have wanted with all that goofy stuff?

Lucie glared at him. "Sheesh! I can't believe your stupid interrogation about underpants couldn't wait until I was done with my bath. I can't believe you. Will you get out of here, please?"

His mind whirling, Ian stepped back. "Fine."

He was so confused, there was nothing else he could think to do.

LATER, MUCH LATER, Lucie deigned to come downstairs. She'd brushed her hair into a ponytail, found a pink T-shirt and a denim jumper, and thrown on her favorite collection of five or six vintage bangle bracelets. After squirting on a tiny bit of perfume, she decided she was ready to face Ian.

She could also smell food, as if he were scrounging up things in her kitchen. Coffee, definitely. And something with cinnamon.

She told herself that if it weren't for the fact that she was starving, she would've let him stew longer. Good grief. What a dope. She'd only let him stay in the first place on sufferance, and then he'd invaded her bath!

The creep had actually waved her beautiful underwear designs in the air, called them kinky, and stared at her breasts in the bathtub. Could he *be* any more obnoxious? He deserved to be spanked.

Spanked. In a pair of bikini briefs. *Oh, yeah.* He would fill a pair of those out like nobody's business.

Her face flushing with warmth, Lucie almost stumbled on the fourth step down. Okay, now wait just a second. Where did that overpowering mental image come from? She'd worked up a good head of steam being mad at him, and all of a sudden she was lost in a fantasy of how good he'd look in her teeniest bikini briefs and how his firm rump would feel if she spanked him.

She lifted a hand to cover her eyes. She was not being herself. *Back to the righteous indignation,* she ordered herself. *You know, the part about how he had no right to malign your underwear designs when he would fill them out so well himself.*

No, that wasn't it. *Anger,* she commanded. *Find your anger. You are a professional. You design underwear. You don't have to think about Ian anywhere near your underwear.*

But Ian out of the underwear was as dangerous as Ian in it. She was losing it, she thought wildly. Her brain kept feeding her visions of Ian, grinning, beautiful, sexy as hell, jumping in and out of his pants.

As she tried not to stagger into the breakfast nook, he sat serenely at the table, pretending to read the newspaper. She noted, however, that he was still on the front page.

He glanced up. "Hello, Lucie. Did you have a nice bath? Are you feeling rested?"

Oh, right. He was *not* calm, no matter what he was faking. But she could play this game.

"I'm feeling much better, thank you. So, what've you cooked up?" She bent over to investigate. There was a pot of coffee at his elbow, plus he'd toasted cinnamon raisin toast and found jars of strawberry preserves and peanut butter.

Hanging onto her frayed nerves, she decided there was nothing remotely upsetting about this peaceful, innocuous breakfast scene. But then he licked a little extra jam off his index finger, carelessly, nonchalantly, his pink tongue flicking at the red streak of strawberry preserves. And she felt her whole body flood with hot color as scarlet as the jam.

Jam. Peanut butter. Somehow they got all mixed up in her mind with bikini briefs. Suddenly her mind filled with all the things you could do with Ian Mackintosh on a rainy afternoon involving peanut butter, jelly and skimpy underwear...

Oh, God. She was dying. Lucie grabbed for the coffeepot, sloshing liquid into a cup with a shaky hand, not bothering with cream or sugar.

"Desperate for a caffeine fix, huh?"

"Yeah, desperate." She gulped it down, scalding her throat, not even caring. At least the choking sensation took her mind off all those other bad things she didn't want to think about.

"Hungry?" he asked innocently, lifting the plate of toast, waving his hand over the jars he'd set out.

"Yes. No. I mean, yes." She was starving. But her mouth went dry. Could she really put peanut butter or jam in her mouth after what she'd just been thinking of doing with it? She grabbed a piece of dry toast and started to chew it.

"You're eating it plain?"

"I like it plain."

"If you don't like the choices, you could look for something else." His gaze was level and curious, as if he were dying to ask what her problem was. Or maybe just what Pandora's Boxers were for. She *had* promised to come down and explain it all. "Your cupboards were pretty bare, though. Except for this, all I saw was a box of macaroni and cheese."

Gazing in the direction of her cupboards, Lucie said vaguely, "Yeah, I needed to get to the store, but didn't have time before the wedding. But then I thought I'd have all day Sunday. Best-laid plans..." she began, wishing immediately she hadn't said the word *laid* or that his dark eyebrow hadn't raised when she did.

"Best-laid plans, huh? Is that how you're describing your fling thing?"

Cretin. "I'm doing my best not to describe it at all," she said tartly. She crunched into her dry toast before she accidentally said anything worse.

"So. Pandora and her boxers." Ian paused. "Are you interested in explaining?"

"I want you to know, this is really none of your business." Pulling up a chair, Lucie topped off her coffee cup and took another long swig, shuddering as the caffeine filtered through her system. "After you burst into my bathroom and got all fussy that way, like some caveman or something, I really shouldn't tell you."

Ian tilted his head to one side. "So why are you going to?"

"Because..." Why was she? Because her underwear had thrown him off-balance, and she liked it. Because she wanted to keep him that way. "Because I am not ashamed of Pandora's Boxers. I think they're beautiful and destined for great success. I also think," she argued, warming up now, "that they would fit you perfectly, so all your nonsense about porn stars and Chippendales dancers and stuffing with socks is just that—nonsense."

Okay, maybe she shouldn't have said that. The tips of his ears got pink, and she found herself dying to steal glances at his crotch. It was like a cartoon, where every time she looked at him, he magically appeared wearing nothing but underpants. Blue ones, red ones, pink ones. Big ones, little ones, very, very little ones...

Not smart, Lucie.

"Maybe you should forget that last part," she added, shoving her chair around the other way. Anything rather than look directly at him. "The story of Pandora's Boxers starts with my mother, whose name was Pandora. Her dream was to design lingerie."

"I suppose everyone needs a dream," he said thoughtfully. He moved his own chair so that he was back squarely in her line of vision. "And hers was to design men's underpants?"

"No, lingerie," she returned. "My mother was only into ladies' lingerie." She raised a hand to forestall his objection. "The briefs and boxers came later. Anyway, as I was saying, my mother started with a dream to create comfortable, flattering bras, corsets, camisoles, that sort of thing, for full-figured women, with lots of support but no wires or bones or stays."

"Full-figured, huh?"

Were his eyes glued to her chest or was that her imagination? Who knew what he was doing over there? Lucie crossed her arms just to be sure. "Right. Full figures. My dad—since you've met him, I don't think this is going to come as any surprise—did not appreciate her goal to design underwear. He thought it was trashy. But she didn't care. She went for it, anyway."

She tried to decipher Ian's expression. Did he, like her father, think it was stupid? She told herself she didn't care. She and her mother knew what was important: the dream.

"Go on," Ian prompted with a hint of mischief in his voice. "I can't wait to hear what comes next."

"Pandora's Boxers were a big hit, right from the start." Lucie shrugged. "A huge hit."

"And then what happened?"

"After she made a pile of money, you mean? Well," she related, ticking items off on her fingers, "her success in the underwear biz screwed up her marriage royally, she and my father got divorced, he remarried Ginetta the Wicked Witch and they had Steffi, I lived with my mom and learned how to sew little camisoles and tap pants at her knee, my mom died, and that was the end of that."

He looked confused at end of the rapid recitation.

"The end of Pandora's Boxers? So you're saying all that stuff in the guest room is twenty years old?"

"Heavens, no." Lucie frowned, scooting around in her seat. "Weren't you paying attention? My mother only did ladies' lingerie. But I... Well, *my* dream is to resurrect *her* dream. And I thought, why not add a men's line, too? Why should overendowed *women* be the only ones who get the right foundation garments?"

There was a long pause on Ian's end of the table. His ears were pink again. "I thought you were a teacher. Now you're saying you're an underwear designer for men with large, uh, equipment?"

Was he making fun? She gave him a wary glance, but he seemed to be sincerely perplexed. He'd better be. As she remembered the size of his, uh, equipment, she thought that he better than anyone should appreciate the need for her product.

"Okay," she explained, "I *am* a teacher. But I have the summers off. I keep a sewing room right next to your room, the guest room, I mean. So I work on my designs there, especially in the summer."

"This is something you'd like to have as your career, but you can't make a go of it?" he asked slowly, as if he were catching on.

"Yes. That's it," she said with more enthusiasm. "It's like a hobby, but I'd love to make it my career. In the meantime, the teaching is a good cover for my father, who still hates the whole idea of Pandora's Boxers. He has this thing about being embarrassed in front of other men—I'm not sure if it humiliated him because my mom was making more money than he was, or because she was out in public, talking about boosting your cleavage and rounding your derriere."

"I guess I can understand that."

"Oh, please. It's so ridiculous!" Rising to her feet, Lucie paced back and forth in the breakfast nook. She was too frazzled to sit in one place anymore, especially across a table from Ian and his damn equipment. "By all rights, it shouldn't be his company to be embarrassed by, anyway," she maintained, launching into an argument that was so familiar she didn't really have to focus to make it. "I'm sure my mother planned to leave the company to me—she always told me it was my legacy. But she was never the most practical person, and who knew she was going to ski into a tree in St. Moritz when I was twelve?"

Ian's forehead crinkled with concentration. "Wait a minute," he said slowly. "Your dad owns Pandora's Boxers now? Your mother left it to him?"

"I'm afraid so." She sat back down. "When my mother died, it turned out she'd never updated her will from when she was still married to my dad. So he got Pandora's Boxers along with everything else."

"That hardly seems fair."

"Tell me about it. But I was only twelve. What was I going to do?" Lucie chewed her lip. She thought she detected a certain sympathy in Ian's eyes. "My Aunt Penny, my mother's sister, said she would contest the will on my behalf, which freaked my dad out. If she didn't, if she let it be, he promised to hold onto Pandora's Boxers for me until I was old enough to run it myself."

"So what's the problem? Why hasn't he turned over the company by now?" he asked, pulling his chair closer to hers.

"I made the mistake of telling him about these great ideas I had—first stretch velour bras for busty women and then the brixers with an extra big pocket for well-endowed men. That was really my breakthrough idea," she explained, leaning nearer in her eagerness to convince him.

"What's a brixer?"

"Oh." Sliding the knife out of the peanut butter, Lucie drew a rough picture for him on a plain piece of toast. "I couldn't really find a good name for them, so I made up my own. See, they're fitted like a brief, only with longer legs. You've seen them, right?"

"Uh, yeah."

When she looked up, his head was right next to hers, as he bent closer to see her sketch. "My dad..." Why was it so hard to concentrate with him so close? She licked her lips, letting the peanut butter knife dangle in her other hand. "My dad had a fit," she said slowly. "He told me that a desire to design underpants proves I'm too immature to run the company."

Ian's hot gaze flickered over her lips. "So there is no Pandora's Boxers anymore?"

"He's turned it into an underwire bra factory." Doodling, Lucie twirled her index finger through the thick design on the toast, not at all sure what she was saying or doing anymore. A fog had descended over her brain. Oops. Now she was stuck with a finger full of peanut butter she didn't know what to do with. "Underwire bras," she repeated awkwardly. "My mother would've hated that."

But Ian did something she didn't expect. He smiled. He caught her hand in his, he brought it to his lips, and he sucked every tiny bit of peanut butter off her finger.

Lucie's mouth fell open. She couldn't breathe.

"I'm thinking we can do each other a big favor," he said in a warm, honeyed tone that slid right down her backbone.

"A f-favor?"

"A one-for-one deal. You help me get rid of Steffi, and I help you get Pandora's Boxers back."

She stared at her finger, still wet from his mouth. "How?"

"You and me, together."

She recalled saying almost exactly those same words to Baker Burns less than twenty-four hours ago, and look what a mess that turned into. "I don't think—"

"Your part would be figuring out how to get Steffi to dump Kyle," Ian overrode her. "You come up with that part of the plan, and I'll help you get Pandora's Boxers from your dad." He smiled again, like a fox just emerging from a henhouse. He might as well have had feathers sticking to his lips.

Hiding her whole hand under the table, Lucie shook her head, trying to clear it. Again, she asked, "How?"

"Your father keeps telling you he'll turn over the company once you prove you're mature enough." Ian leaned back in his chair, balancing it on two legs. "I know men like your father. When he says he wants to see proof that you're mature, he means you have a guy around to bail you out—as in, a guy he approves of."

She hated to admit it, but he *was* right. How many times had she heard her dad sing Steffi's praises for nabbing a great husband candidate and settling down? Still, Lucie had a very good idea where Ian was going with this, and she didn't like it one bit.

"So what more," he said slyly, "could he want than me?"

Lucie stood, turning away. "You're not serious."

"I'm eligible, aren't I?" he argued, coming after her. "Clearly I have a certain business acumen, so he can't object on those grounds. What was that you said about the perfect Ken doll with all the accessories? Barbie's Dream Family, isn't that what you called it?"

"Well, yes, but I hardly meant—"

But Ian was off and running. "So we're agreed that I'm presentable. Not to mention the fact that after this morning, he already thinks we're an item, so there's a credibility factor."

"I never suggested that you wouldn't pass muster," she broke in, getting aggravated. "But why would you want to? I know I'm not your type." He started to object, but she held him off. "Please. I've seen Feather. I know what you're looking for. Someone young, beautiful, simple, and very temporary. That isn't me."

He rose, advancing on her, until he had her backed into the wall, one strong arm on each side, and he was staring her right in the eyes. "We do have a certain chemistry. That works to our advantage."

"Chemistry?" Lucie stared at his collarbone. "I—I don't think so."

"Oh, come on. Last night—"

"I don't remember any of it. Not a single minute," she insisted.

"Not even one?" He dipped his head, pressing his warm, soft lips to the nape of her neck.

Lucie closed her eyes, trying really hard not to moan. Hell, of course she remembered. Far more than she wanted to. But she wasn't going to tell him that. Not even if he sucked her finger, or kissed her, or started to unbutton her...

"Stop that!" She smacked his hands away from her blouse.

"I think I just proved my case. Chemistry," he said with satisfaction.

"You probably have chemistry with a cardboard box. Like that thing with the peanut butter just now." Angrily, she demanded, "Who wouldn't start to melt when you suck their finger?"

"I have lots more tricks with peanut butter," he murmured. "Wanna try?"

"I knew it!" Waving her hands in the air, she changed the subject before he sandbagged her again. "It doesn't matter. I still say I'm not your type." Hastily, she added, "And you're not mine, either."

"I believe you," he said easily. "You just turned thirty, so I'll bet you're past ready to settle down. You want the house, kids, sheepdog, minivan, blah, blah, blah."

"Gee, you make it sound so attractive." Too bad he

was absolutely wrong. Sure, she wanted to settle down. But she wanted a romantic, reliable, caring man first, not to mention some *fun*.

If and when she found this mystery man... Well, the rest of it could wait. Sheepdog? Minivan? Not on your life. She had trips to Paris and walks in the rain and sonnets by moonlight at the top of her agenda. Not that Ian Mackintosh knew the first thing about any of that. All he knew was one-nighters with whipped cream and a cherry on top...

She squeezed her eyes shut. Okay, that wasn't fair. He hadn't mentioned whipped cream or cherries. No, that was her fertile imagination.

"Don't take it personally," he said, insinuating his body against hers. "No one is my type if we're talking long-term. Because I don't—talk long-term, I mean."

"Given that fact, do you really want people thinking you're in a relationship with me?" Lucie ducked under his arm, desperate to put a few inches between them. "Won't that sort of ruin your reputation?"

"Half the people I know already think I am in a relationship with you. Why would I care now?"

"No, half the people you know think you had one night of bad judgment, one night of crazed, greased-weasel sex—"

But he ran roughshod over her words, striding up behind her, breathing on her neck from back there. "Lucie, it will probably do my reputation good for people to think I'm in a real, live relationship. And to tell you the truth, I haven't got anything better to do. I'm basically sitting around waiting for a check to get mailed. In the meantime, nobody cares much where I am or what I'm doing or who I'm doing it with."

She held herself very still. "Don't you think that's sad?"

"Maybe." He was close enough that when he lifted his shoulders in an eloquent shrug, she could feel it. "I may as well be your live-in lover, especially if it helps untangle my brother and get your company back."

"Live-in lover?" she echoed in horror, batting at his hands, wheeling on him. "That's what you want?"

"That's my plan." He looped his arms around her waist, yanking her up against him. "That's the quickest way to convince people. If I stay."

Again, his mouth found her neck. She could feel the hot puff of his breath against her ear when he whispered, "Here, with you."

6

LUCIE FELT FAINT. As if she would ever agree to Ian moving in with her, even for a few hours, even if her spine did feel like spaghetti. Even if he was, as he had reminded her, the perfect Ken doll, complete with accessories.

And then it hit her.

"Damn it," she swore out loud. Breaking away from him, she put both hands over her temples, unable to stop the thoughts from forming.

"What is it? Why do you look like your head's going to explode?"

Frowning, she kept her new discovery to herself, muttering under her breath. Could she tell him? Could she *not*?

"Lucie," he said with alarm. "Are you all right?"

Finally, she came out with it. "No, I'm not all right. But I do know how to get Steffi to dump your brother."

"What? How?" he asked eagerly.

Lucie shrugged and shook her head. "I can't believe I'm saying this, but I just realized the one sure way to make Steffi dump Kyle..."

"Yes?"

"Is for you to move in with me."

Ian stopped, narrowing his eyes. "Oh, really?"

"Really," she admitted. "It's what you said, about the perfect Ken doll. You, and Kyle. You're both like that."

He shoved his hands in his pockets. "Is that good or bad?"

"That's good. At least for this plan." She explained, "I told you before that Steffi hates to share her toys. And if you and I are supposedly together, well, it's as if I've got an exact copy of her favorite doll—a doll in the same family, with the same blue-ribbon connections and lovely house and oodles of charm."

"Thank you. I think."

"It really has very little to do with you," she noted abruptly, not at all pleased with her own conclusion, not at all sure she was going to be able to handle this. "It has to do with Steffi not wanting to share her toy *or* his Dream Family, especially with me."

"So rather than share him...?"

"My guess is that she will throw him out," she told him succinctly. "Which, by the way, is exactly what she did when my dad gave us both cashmere sweaters for Christmas one year. She cut hers to ribbons rather than be caught dead in the same sweater I had. A smarter girl might've cut *mine* to ribbons. But not Steffi. If I had it, its value plummeted enough that she wanted no part of it."

Ian ran a hasty hand through his hair, leaving short tufts sticking up here and there. But his blue eyes were alight with anticipation. "So I'm moving in for a few days, we're flaunting ourselves at your dad and Steffi, and killing two birds with one stone. Excellent."

Why did she hate so much giving in and agreeing with him? "I have a condition."

"Let's hear it."

"You may pretend to be my live-in lover, but you will not *be* my live-in lover," she said clearly. "No hanky-panky. None of this cuddly stuff or groping or even breathing on me."

One dark eyebrow arched. "That's a little harsh, don't you think?"

"No, I don't. We had our fling. That's it, no more."

"And this is necessary because...?"

"Because I'm not like you. You may think carefree rolls in the hay are just ducky, but I'm not like that." *Jeez.* She hated to sound all Rebecca of Sunnybrook Farm, especially when the barn door was already wide open and the horse long gone, but... But a person had to have some way to keep her sanity, didn't she? "Ian, I'm not going to lie to you. The fling was one thing. It was my birthday, I was depressed, I lost my mind temporarily. But if I plan to sleep with someone, you know, on a regular basis, then I need certain things. I need—"

"Wait, don't tell me," he said in a sardonic tone. "Commitment, trust and respect. Am I right?"

"Well, yes. But don't worry—I'm not looking for that from you," she assured him. "As if any woman with a brain would look for those things from you."

His mood went grim at that, but good grief, he'd said it himself, hadn't he? He obviously wasn't in the market for a real relationship, one that involved heads and minds and...well, anything that wasn't just south in the anatomy.

"What's the matter?" she asked sweetly. "Afraid you can't handle keeping your pants on?"

"Please." His eyes narrowed. "I can handle it. I'm not so sure about you, though. You're the one who gets turned on if you're even breathed on. Isn't that what you said?"

"No, it isn't." Maybe it was. She didn't remember anymore. "If you think about it," Lucie remarked, plowing onward before she tripped up, "my stipulation is a good thing. With no sex games, you can be sure that I'm not trying to trap you into another Webster-Mackintosh marital alliance. Not after we saw how well it worked for Steffi and Kyle."

He chewed on that one for a bit. "You're hardly Steffi and I'm not Kyle."

"It doesn't matter. It would never work between you and me, anyway. We're clear on that. And I feel guilty enough about our one night together to even think about two nights or three nights—"

"Maybe a week, week and a half," he finished for her with a wicked gleam in his eye.

Lucie didn't want to contemplate how bizarre this was going to be, living under the same roof with this infuriating, controlling, drop-dead sexy man. *Think about Pandora's Boxers*, she told herself. *But not on Ian. Instead, think about horrid Steffi and poor Kyle.*

It was too late. Mentally, she was already back in the place where her sinful briefs and boxers did a tap dance on and off Ian's body.

Her voice was shaky when she said, "A week is way too long. We'll just have to make it work quicker than that. If we get in Steffi's face, I really think she'll run to get rid of Kyle."

"And I really think your father will run to give you back your company," Ian announced, offering his hand to shake. "Do we have a deal?"

Lucie took it, ignoring the electricity that zipped through her arm when his warm, strong fingers encircled hers. *If you get back Pandora's Boxers, and you get one over on Steffi, this will all be worth it.* Taking a deep breath, she declared, "Deal."

STAYING WITH LUCIE was making him insane. Given the fact that it was his idea, Ian supposed he deserved every frustrating minute.

Meanwhile, the plan wasn't even working. Although they'd invited all their targets over to the cottage to witness the supposed love match up close and personal, the invitations had been declined post haste.

Other than that, Ian was left cooling his heels. Sure, he'd arranged a tow truck and a new windshield for Lucie's Jeep. And he'd moved some things into her place, just so he had a few changes of clothes and his own, non-girly soap and shampoo. But after that was accomplished, they were just getting on each other's nerves as they waited for her strange relatives to notice that they were now a couple.

So last night Lucie had gotten more direct and appeared on the Websters' doorstep with a gift in hand, professing her abject apologies for the wedding-morning-after mess. Steffi was even there when she arrived. While Ginetta said she didn't care to hear anything Lucie had to say and, no, she wouldn't let her speak to her father, Lucie reported that Steffi swept by on her way out the door.

"Why aren't you off on your honeymoon?" Lucie asked with feigned innocence.

"Don't even talk to me," Steffi returned coldly. "As if I would believe for a minute that you and *Ian* were really together. He is so out of your league. Don't worry—no matter what pranks you pull, I'm ecstatic and I'm going to stay that way."

And then Steffi had jumped into her brand-new red convertible—a wedding gift from Kyle, she declared—and spun gravel as she sped off to her brand-new house.

When Lucie related the story to Ian, he had only one comment. "New car? She's already bleeding him dry."

"I tried to warn you."

"I tried to warn *him*." Ian shook his head. "Love. Men are such idiots when they fall in love."

So far, their attempts to be cheerfully, and fraudulently, in love had elicited no response whatsoever. Which meant that Ian had been living in the same house with the hottest woman he'd ever met and not even touched her. For forty-eight of the most excruciating hours of his life.

Dropping the newspaper to the floor, Ian sank further into Lucie's red velvet sofa, debating how long they should wait before they gave up and concluded their plan was a failure. Damn it, anyway. He wasn't ready to give up yet. He wasn't ready to repack his bags and find somewhere else to live while he waited for the much-delayed sale of m-tosh.com to go through.

His life was on hold, and while it was, he wanted to spend his time driving Lucie crazy—unless she and her platonic plans drove him there first.

"Lucie?" he called out. "Got any brilliant ideas on how to make this relationship look more authentic?"

"No." She marched into the living room carrying a laundry basket, all smart and snappy in a pair of beige capri pants and an oversize white shirt. She'd pulled her hair back again, and she had an armful of colorful bracelets like she always did, those bracelets that made a clinking, clanking sound before she entered the room. But she frowned at him. "Could you please sit up and clean up those newspapers?"

He was suddenly struck by the fact that they behaved more like an old married couple than any old married couple he knew. Here he was, lounging on the couch, reading the newspaper, while she washed clothes. Not to mention that they had no sex life. All they needed was a dog and a baby and they could have their own sitcom.

Good lord. He'd never have imagined himself falling into this stereotype without a whimper. Jumping to his feet, he crammed the newspapers into a pile and tried to think of something—anything—nondomestic that he could do.

Before he had a chance to come up with anything, the doorbell rang loudly. He thought that was probably the first time since he'd been at Lucie's that he'd even heard it.

"Do you mind getting that?" She sat on the floor with her basket and started lifting out briefs and "brixers."

Okay, so she wasn't doing laundry, just sorting her inventory. "What are you, indexing by size?" he asked as he crossed to the door. He opened it, expecting a delivery or something similar, but instead found a huge guy, at least six-six, college age maybe, with shoulders so wide they barely fit in the door.

"Hey," the kid said, balancing one beefy arm on the doorframe. "Lucie in?"

Ian barely had time to open his mouth before Lucie called out, "In here, Toby! You're a few minutes early. Did you bring T-Bone, too?"

"Yeah, he's in the car. He's comin'."

"Is that a dog? Or is there actually a person in the world named T-Bone?" Ian asked idly, as another behemoth joined the first one inside the door. Except for the fact that Toby had a buzz cut and his friend had long hair dangling about his stubby face, they could've been twins. Huge, none-too-bright twins.

Toby and T-Bone stood in the living room, a little clumsy, gazing expectantly at Lucie, not in the least threatened by the fact that Ian was there. But then, why should they be? They were twice his size, in width if not height.

But then the first one gave Ian a beady stare. "Hey, Lucie, this guy's not, um, staying, you know, during, is he?"

"Not if you're uncomfortable with that," she answered kindly.

Toby elbowed his friend and they both giggled in a kind of heh-heh-heh way.

Ian lowered his voice as he bent in behind Lucie. "Who are these bozos? Your pool boys?"

"I don't have a pool," she responded, her face a study in concentration as she draped and redraped underwear over the furniture.

"Oh, no. Don't tell me." Carefully, he asked, "The beefcake boys don't have anything to do with Pandora's Boxers, do they?"

"Uh-huh. They're my models." She smiled absently at the two giants. "Toby and T-Bone are football players. They answered an ad I put in their college newspaper asking for full-figured male models."

"I'll just bet they did." He had half a mind to tell her that anyone pumping that many steroids was probably underequipped in the area she needed, but he kept his mouth shut.

"So they're going to try on a few pairs of Pandora's Boxers and let me check out how things fit on a real person instead of just a dummy," she said brightly.

Once again, he kept his mouth shut, although that line about trying things out on dummies was awfully hard to ignore.

"And then," Lucie went on, "not today, but later, after I've got the right fit, I've hired a photographer to take some shots for my Internet, um, platform." She smiled, her most perfect, sunny smile, as Ian got a very bad feeling in the pit of his stomach.

He couldn't stop himself from pointing out, "It's called a Web site, and you don't have one."

"I know. But I'm hiring another college kid to make one for me." She picked up a pair of short black trunks with lightning bolts on them, rising from the floor and raising her voice at the same time. "Toby, I'd like you to try these first. And T-Bone, what do you think of the fruit-motif bikini briefs? The peaches go on the back and the banana goes in the front."

And where else would peaches and bananas go? T-Bone's giggles got louder, and Toby nudged him harder. They were both grinning like morons.

Ian began to simmer. Steam wasn't far off. "Lucie, can I speak to you in the kitchen?"

"Sure. Guys, you can take these back to the sewing room to change. First door on the left." As they toddled off, the tiny underwear disappearing into their massive fists, Lucie turned to Ian. "What is it?"

"This is a really bad idea."

"What part of it?" She tipped her head to one side. "The photos? The Web site?"

"Using these big boneheads to model your briefs," he said tersely. As if she didn't know. "They're huge, they're probably pumped up on steroids, they probably lied about the, uh, size requirements, and you're putting them in a sexually charged situation. You can tell they're already planning their letter to Penthouse about the foxy older woman who invited them over to pose in skimpy underwear and how it turned into a threesome."

"What?" she asked with a gasp. "Jeez, Ian, even for you, that's out there."

"You're putting yourself in a dangerous position, Lucie."

She shrugged. "If you're that worried, you can stick around to protect me."

"Thank God I *am* here. But did you notice Toby asked if I was leaving? And even if I'm here, do you really think I could defend you *or* me against those guys? They could crush me like a twig."

"Oh, come on, Ian. Quit being ridiculous." She swished her ponytail from side to side as she regarded him with something like pity. "Sexually charged situation. I can't believe you said that."

"What else can it be when you stick big hunks of meat in very small drawers?" he shot back.

"It's nothing like that. I'm a professional. They're just models," she argued.

"All right then." Even he couldn't believe the words coming out of his mouth. "Send the beefcake boys home and I'll model Pandora's Boxers for you."

Lucie's eyes widened. "You will not!"

"Yes, I will."

"Absolutely not." Her cheeks grew pink, and she avoided his eyes. "No way."

"Why not?" He started to feel a little better about this. "If it's not a sexually charged situation, why should you care if it's them or me?"

"If it's you, it will be," she countered, crossing her arms over her white blouse.

He knew it was a defensive gesture, but all it did was

remind him of the sumptuous curves she was hiding. And make him argue his points that much more strenuously. There was no way he was going to lie down and let those thick-necked dolts get near Lucie's curves. And he realized suddenly that he knew exactly how to get her out of the line of fire.

"You know, Lucie, you're the one who laid down the no-touch rules between you and me. So far, I haven't come near you. But you're still afraid, aren't you?" His lips curved in a provocative smile. "Not that I'm going to touch you, but vice versa. You think if you put me in your boxers, *you* can't handle it. You'll be all over me like white on rice. That's it, isn't it?"

"No. Of course I can handle it," she scoffed.

"Then why don't you boot Frankenstein and his brother and let me do the modeling?" he asked, crossing his own arms over his chest. "You said yourself that your designs would fit me. I dare you to put your briefs where your mouth was."

The pink in her cheeks took on an even rosier hue and the very mouth he'd mentioned parted slightly, as if she were having trouble breathing.

Okay, so the line about putting her briefs where her mouth was had come out even more suggestive than he'd intended. They both knew her mouth *had* been there, even if she refused to admit she remembered. *He* remembered. And he wasn't planning on parting with that memory anytime soon.

"Well?" he prompted. "Can you handle it, Lucie?"

"Of course I can. I told you, this is business to me." Her eyes were on his, quite firmly, as if she were afraid to go any lower. "I look at men's underwear every day."

"Okay then. The boys are out of here, and I'm in. Right?"

"Right," she said, inhaling sharply. "Right."

"Hey, guys," Ian called out immediately. "You can put your clothes back on. Lucie changed her mind."

The two of them came hurtling out of the guest room like rockets on the launch pad, already fully dressed in their street clothes.

"Lucie, we're sorry, but this didn't work," Toby announced, his wide face wrinkled with disappointment. "We both tried 'em on and they're too tight in the abs and quads for anyone who spends any time in a weight room."

"Thighs and waist," Ian translated.

"And the front part..." Toby clammed up, but his friend chimed in.

"The front part sucks, man," T-Bone growled. "I mean, my banana just kind of hung there, you know? More like a yellow raisin, man. That sucks."

"Well, that was more than I needed to know," Ian whispered in her ear.

"Right." Her face was a major shade of red. "Sorry, Toby, T-Bone, but you're right. I guess I'll go back to the drawing board."

"Appreciate your help," Ian added, going to the door. He stayed where he was, stubbornly holding the door, until Toby and T-Bone had both left.

Once they were gone, he said quickly, "All right,

let's get to the bedroom and throw away whatever they wore."

"Oh, come on! I really like the fruity ones. Can't I just wash them?"

"Will washing get rid of any memory that T-Bone's been in them?"

"Good point."

He took one look at her face and she glanced at him and they both started to laugh.

"I hate it when you're right," she managed around her giggles. "'My banana hung there like a raisin.' Good grief!"

Ian was feeling pretty proud of himself, having vanquished the two morons so easily. But he lost a bit of his bravado when Lucie sobered, giving him the once-over.

Briskly, she inquired, "So, when would you like to get started? I still need some fittings, you know."

He could've argued that it wasn't his fault Toby and T-Bone didn't work out, so he shouldn't have to replace them. But he didn't. He recognized an opening gambit when he heard one. And he knew how to slam the ball back into her court. Staring her down, he asked, "Which ones do you want to see?"

"Got a preference?"

"You pick."

"Okay." She tapped a finger against her mouth. "How do you feel about a thong?"

He smiled. Nice bluff, but he knew there were no thongs among her stock. "Sure. Why not?" He paused. "Oh, I forgot. You don't have any."

"Too bad. Hmm... Let's see. All right." Her gaze held him, and he realized again that Lucie had moxie. She wasn't going to back down any more than he was. After a long pause, after sweat began to break out on his forehead, she said, "There's a pair of low-rise, black velvet brixers in a drawer in your room. They're one of my newest designs. They've got a silver moon on the back and a star on the front. In my living room. Five minutes."

"It won't take me five minutes."

"Good." She gave him a determined smile. "I'll be ready."

"Good. So will I."

THIS WAS A dangerous game they were playing.

As Ian stalked off to her guest room to look for the black pants, Lucie sagged against the back of the couch. What the hell had she just done?

"You're out of your mind," she murmured, blowing stray tendrils off her forehead. She was overheated and overstimulated and she was suffering from lack of oxygen. That would explain it.

"It's not my fault if I have a hard time backing down from a dare," she complained out loud, scooting over to the refrigerator and plucking out a few ice cubes. She slid one over her forehead, enjoying the frigid shock, and dunked two more down inside her collar. "He dared me. He said I couldn't handle it. What could I do?"

You could've been sensible and laughed at him or at least put him in really long, baggy pajama bottoms.

"That would be like letting him win," she argued with herself. But she heard the muffled sound of footsteps coming back down the hall.

Frantic, she quickly pressed the ice against each cheek then tossed it into the sink. Then she raced back to the living room, pulled a pad of paper and a measuring tape out of the bottom of the laundry basket, and leaped onto the couch.

She could hear him rounding the corner as she scrambled to situate herself on the sofa, legs neatly crossed, pad and tape in hand. She worked on manufacturing a studious—maybe even bored—expression to greet him.

Damn the man. He didn't even look flustered.

She kept her eyes securely on his face, but his smug smile told her he knew exactly what she was doing.

You think I'm too much of a coward to look below the waist? she telegraphed.

Bring it on, his expression dared her.

Fine. Here goes. Pressing her lips into a tight line, Lucie stood. She looped her gaze down there, flitting over his wide shoulders, that smooth, finely sculpted chest, his hard abs, the tiny scar running from his belly button down to the low-slung black velvet line where the fabric began...

Okay, that was enough. Focusing on a point on the wall beyond his hip, she bent her head to one side, murmuring, "Hmm... Looks like that pair fits pretty well."

"Pretty well," he agreed.

Damn him. He was enjoying this. She made him behave like beef on the hoof, like a total and complete sex object, and he enjoyed it!

She circled around behind him, tangling and untangling the tape measure, raking her eyes up and down, letting herself drink him in and swoon all at once, now that he couldn't see her. He was *fine*. Broad shouldered, slim through the torso and hips, he had these adorable little buns, all high and tight and perky there in the back of the snug pants, with a shiny silver crescent moon riding one curve. *Oh, yeah.*

Her trademark "brixers" fit like a glove to mid-thigh, the low waistband barely clinging to his hips, the stretchy velvet hugging him, outlining every flexed muscle. Her palms itched to reach out and grab a hunk of flesh. She couldn't believe the carnal, lascivious, lustful things she was thinking.

And when her fingers curled, uncurled, edged closer as if they had a mind of their own...

"Are you pinching my butt?" he demanded.

"Of course not," she said in a rush. "Just, uh, pointing out the pocket. Did you see the pocket?" Tucking two fingers down the silver-edged patch on the outside of his thigh, she noted breezily, "It's for your cell phone. That way, if your pants—your outer pants, I mean—don't have any pockets, you can just set your phone on vibrate and store it right here."

"Got it. Vibrating my thigh. Great idea." He glanced down at her, his gaze cynical. "Are you about done?"

Quickly, she composed herself, pulling her fingers out of his seductive little pocket and making her face a blank. She hoped.

"Done?" she repeated. "Oh, no. Not nearly." Flicking her tape measure like a whip, Lucie dropped to her knees in front of him. "I need to measure your inseam."

Her words came out all wispy and weird. She didn't mean for it to sound that way—in fact, she was going for a no-nonsense, brisk tone—but somehow her voice got stuck on the way out. With her head only inches from the rather dramatic bulge in his fly—no mere raisin hanging here—she closed her eyes and poked her tape right up in there.

He sucked in his breath when she made contact, but he didn't lose any ground. "How can you measure with your eyes closed?" he muttered.

So she opened them. But she wasn't looking at the measuring tape or even the inseam. She was staring dead ahead, at the extra-large pouch, covered with a gleaming silver star, that was her creation, her brainstorm.

She felt faint—she really could see a whole fleet of silver stars in the periphery of her vision—as she gazed at the long, hard, undeniable proof that Ian was made to fill out her briefs. And then some. Her mouth went dry and her temperature soared and she absolutely, positively could not move.

With a muffled oath, Ian set his hands on her shoulders, clasped her, pulled her up, and slashed his mouth over hers. She could feel his heat and his fierce, irresistible passion, the pent-up force of his frustration and desire as she melted into the kiss. Mindless, itchy, on fire, she pressed up and into him, ready for more.

He broke away to gasp for breath. "All right, I give," he said savagely. "Somebody has to do it. And it might as well be me. I want you. I want your mouth on me. Now."

She was already reaching for the thin layer of black velvet and that tantalizing star as he pushed her to the carpet. Fumbling with her buttons, he showered kisses on her collarbone and her neck and the mounds of her breasts, only partially concealed by her thin knit bra.

They were both frantically peeling away her clothes, nipping at each other's mouths, plunging headfirst into this shocking abyss of pleasure and haste, when the doorbell rang.

"Ignore it," Ian commanded, dragging the scrunchie out of her hair and sending red-gold waves flying every which way. He grabbed a bunch of it, kissed her again, and she fell over on top of him, sliding her hand up and down the front of his starstruck fly.

But the ringing continued.

"Ian! Ian! It's Kyle."

"Him *again*?" Lucie snapped.

"Ignore him," Ian said again, more angrily this time.

"Ian, I know you're in there. I saw you two through the window!" Kyle shouted, pounding the door with a fist to emphasize his words, then rattling the knob. "I'll come in the window if I have to. Steffi is following me. Come on! Open up!"

"Through the window?" Lucie squealed, jumping away, clutching her blouse to her front. "He was watching us? Oh, God, the door's not even locked."

Ian swore, something dark and mean about Kyle's

ability to procreate. Swiftly, he pulled Lucie into his lap on the floor and scrambled to help her put her clothes together.

"I'm going to kill you," he yelled as Kyle came blasting in. "Do you have any idea just how bad your timing is?"

7

"I DON'T CARE how bad my timing is," Kyle shot back, muscling inside, slamming the door behind him. "I'm beyond desperate. I've been living with Steffi for three days. Three *long* days."

"Uh, I lived with her for six years," Lucie put in as she and Ian did a rapid tag team job buttoning her blouse. "I think I appreciate your predicament."

Ian stood up slowly, bringing Lucie with him. His strong, bare arms encircled her, holding her fast, but she didn't have any illusions that this two-man luge routine was for her protection. Naaah. She was just camouflage for him and his skin-tight, black velvet undies.

With a suspicious expression, Kyle grumbled, "You two look like you're having fun, maybe too much fun. Aren't you supposed to be coming up with a way to get me out of this?"

Trying not to blush—again—Lucie concentrated on staying as still as possible and not rubbing against Ian or his provocative bulges. To Kyle, she noted, "Hey, *you're* the one who married her. Some people, less kind than your brother, might tell you you'd made your bed and now it's time to lie in it."

Of course, they might tell her the same thing vis-à-vis sharing a bed with Ian and now lying with him...

Losing her patience, she demanded, "What were you thinking, anyway? Marrying Steffi?"

"If he was thinking at all," Ian said grimly, "it was only with his—"

But Kyle interrupted, "I know, I know." Pacing, he admitted, "It's my own fault. But she pretended to be someone totally different until she hooked me. She was sweet and funny and very considerate. Yeah, she acted spoiled sometimes. But I just thought it was because she was young. How was I supposed to know?"

"I tried to tell you," Ian muttered.

"Sweet, funny and considerate, huh? Boy, she sure had you smoked. I've seen it a million times with my friends." Lucie shook her head sadly. "They have these awful boyfriends and you know it and you can't say a word because they're madly in love and they'll just be mad at you, not the guy. So you think, well, hey, maybe I can do more good keeping my mouth shut and hanging in, so when she needs a friend to get through the fallout, I'll be there." Over her shoulder, she asked Ian, "Is that how it was?"

He just sort of nodded. "That's right," he mumbled, with a very uncomfortable look on his face.

Considering her backside was still plastered to his front, she understood his discomfort.

"I'm sorry," Kyle started in a grumpy tone. "I'm sorry I came busting in here, I'm sorry I walked in on whatever I walked in on, and mostly, I'm sorry I married Steffi. But you guys have to help me. She's pushing this honeymoon hard, and she doesn't believe in my sinus infection."

"Kyle, we understand that you're in a bind. But, you know, if you don't want a honeymoon, you could still follow my first suggestion and break both your legs. And if you keep interrupting us like this," his brother snarled, "I may be willing to do the leg-breaking my-self."

"Hold on." Ignoring Ian, Kyle cocked an ear near the window. "Did you hear that? Steffi's car. She's here. I told you she was following me."

Steffi? Coming here? *Uh-oh.* Lucie exhaled. She knew what that meant. Show time. But, right now, appearing to be a couple wouldn't require any acting.

He stood so close to her, she was melting again. This was becoming a habit. If only he weren't breathing on her neck. If only he could back up a few inches or put on more clothes.

If only Kyle would leave and Steffi would leave and she and Ian could finish what they started... Maybe then she wouldn't be dripping with frustration.

"Where can I hide?" Kyle asked quickly, surveying the room. "Upstairs?"

Just go away so I can seduce your brother!

"You can't hide," Ian told him with disdain. "Didn't you leave your car out front?"

"Oh, yeah. Damn it. Why is she hounding me like this?" He rammed a hand through his short-cropped hair. "I guess she thinks if she pushes me hard enough, I'll do whatever she wants. But I'm not taking her on this honeymoon, and I swear, one more big-ticket item and I *will* divorce her. I don't care if it does screw up m-tosh.com. About five more minutes of Steffi is all I can take."

"What you don't know is that it's good she's here," Ian said urgently. As they heard a car door slam, he yanked Lucie even harder up against him, one hand splayed on her hip, the other looping around her neck, resting above her breast, molding her to him. She felt like ice cream trapped in a heated scoop, getting softer and warmer... "We need her to see us together."

"Ian's right," she whispered, casting nervous glances at the door, reminding herself to breathe, watching Ian's hand rise and fall above her breast every time she did. Their unwanted guests weren't leaving anytime soon, and she needed to hang onto her sanity in the meantime. *Concentrate.* "Us, together, in Steffi's face—it's part of our plan."

"I don't get it." Kyle's eyes skimmed their intimate embrace. "But, okay, if you say so. Meanwhile, what do *I* do?"

"Well," Lucie tried, making a concerted effort to ignore all the physical signals her body was sending, "if you can do it without her knowing, I think you'd better get yourself to a lawyer. I also think..." Were Ian's lips that close to her neck on purpose or was it just an accident? What was he doing to generate all that heat back there? *Whatever you do, Kyle, just don't put on a pair of Pandora's Boxers. Or Steffi will never let you leave.* "I—I mean, I'd go for gooey, whiny, needy—that kind of thing. She'll hate that."

"Gooey, whiny, needy," Kyle repeated.

"Right. You know, like a puppy. A whimpering puppy." Which she felt like at this exact moment. *Think Steffi.* That was better than a cold shower. What else would Steffi hate? "Can you pretend to be poor? Or at least to be having money problems? That way you can cancel her credit cards and close her accounts and tell her it's a cash flow thing." Lucie nodded, on a roll. "That will drive her nuts."

"And whatever you do, don't sleep with her," Ian warned.

Lucie closed her eyes. *Do what I say, not what I do, huh?* If she couldn't relieve her frustration any other way, she was tempted to turn around in his arms, grab him and shake him. But it was too late.

"Hellooo?" Steffi cried from the other side of the door. "Is Kyle here?"

"Lovesick puppy plus cash flow," Ian reminded his brother. "Give us a few seconds and then let Steffi in. Tell her you haven't seen us. Oh, and mention that we're obviously majorly in love."

Snagging Lucie's hand, he pulled her down the hall. She asked, "What are you doing?" but he didn't answer, just unbuttoned her blouse again and messed up her hair.

"Huh?" She looked down at her gaping shirt. "Why did you do that? I thought we might put on more clothes, not ditch what we have left."

"Take off your pants," he whispered.

"Here? In the hall?"

"Shh! Just do it. We have to make it look good."

"What?" But she had somehow turned into Ian's robot. If he wanted her naked in the hallway, so be it. As he put a finger to his lips, indicating silence, she undid her capri pants, so recently refastened, and wiggled out of them. Then she stood there, self-conscious in her open shirt over a Pandora's Boxers knit bra and panties.

Behind them, they heard Kyle say weakly, "Sweetie, what are you doing here?"

"I came to get you," Steffi said in an edgy voice. "What are *you* doing here?"

"Just stopped by to see my brother. When I got here, the door was open but no one seems to be home." He added, in a loud, fake voice, "Ian and I have some business problems we need to discuss. You know, *money* problems."

Okay, so he'd remembered that much of his instructions.

Steffi didn't seem to care, however. "Whatever," she returned peevishly. "If no one's home, then let's get out of here."

"That's our cue," Ian mouthed. "Act passionate."

As she'd predicted, *acting* passionate was not going to be necessary when Ian was around.

To her complete surprise, he swept her up into his arms, started to make King of the Jungle noises, and then hauled her out to the living room. He took her right to the sofa, tossed her down, and threw himself on top of her. He said something in the "Roarrr!" range and started kissing her and nuzzling her neck.

Steffi shrieked, "What's going on here?"

Only then did he feign shock and scramble to a

standing position. "Where did you come from?" he asked in a confused tone, staring slack-jawed at Kyle and Steffi.

Lucie had to hand it to him. He certainly seemed credible. Meanwhile, she sort of froze there in place, not sure what to do—except button her shirt again. No matter what sort of exhibitionist Ian had turned into, she wasn't really into that. Idly, she wondered whether she could sneak out to the hallway behind his back and find her khakis.

"Oh, my. It looks as if Ian and Lucie are majorly in love," Kyle began brightly, sending his brother a broad wink, but Steffi interrupted.

"What are you wearing?" she demanded. "Is that a star on your crotch? Oh, my God."

"Lucie designed them," Ian announced, doing what she supposed was his take on a model's strut. "I love them."

Oh, sure. Only a few minutes ago, he'd pasted Lucie to his front to block the view. *Now* he was modeling.

Steffi's eyes were wide with horror. "It's true. It must be. Only someone crazy enough to be in love with her would wear her bizarre underwear. What, is she drugging you?"

"Steffi?" a gruff voice broke in from the open doorway. "I saw your car. Are you all right?"

"My dad is here?" Lucie groaned, dropping her head to her hands. "Oh, jeez. Who else?"

His younger daughter ran to him. "Daddy! It's terrible! My new brother-in-law is in love with *Lucie*. I saw it with my own eyes!"

It was playing out exactly as they'd planned, and yet somehow, her family still had the power to make her feel inadequate and pathetic. Maybe it would be a good start toward self-respect if she could manage to keep her clothes on around Ian. She swore under her breath.

Standing over her, Ian whispered, "It's okay. This is good. This is what we wanted."

But she begged to differ. "We wanted them to think we're in love, not that we're a couple of lusty lunatics."

"Same difference," Ian murmured.

"Sometimes you are such a guy, you know that?"

But Steffi wasn't finished. "Did you see, Daddy? He's wearing some of her designs—you know, those disgusting Panda Pants or whatever. What am I going to do? I can't be married to someone whose brother is in love with *Lucie*."

"It's obscene," her father growled. He shielded Steffi by pressing her face into his chest. "Lucie, can't you keep your boyfriend out of those underpants?"

Dryly, Lucie noted, "I could, but I don't think you'd like him out of those underpants any better than you like him in them."

"We can't help it if we're in love," Ian offered sweetly. He joined Lucie on the sofa and set an arm around her shoulders. And then he gave her a good lip-smacker of a kiss. "But I understand your concern, sir. She *is* your daughter. If you're thinking of asking what my intentions are, well, we have plans. Big plans. I don't want to say the m-word, but you catch my drift."

"M-word?" Lucie repeated.

"Marriage." He winked at her, squeezing her to cover the tiny squeal she made. But that was nothing compared to Steffi's reaction.

"Marriage?" she shrieked. "But then Lucie will be my sister-in-law!"

"She's already your half sister," Ian reminded her. "Anyway, before we get to the altar, Lucie's dream is to resurrect Pandora's—"

"Oh, no, you don't!" Don Webster shouted, his face reddening and his hands clenching into fists. "Not the damn underwear again. Give it up already. Lucie can't handle it."

The sparkle of good humor in Ian's eyes changed to steely determination. "I think she can," he said flatly. "I love Pandora's Boxers. I also love a challenge. I've promised Lucie we will find a way to make her dream a reality." His narrow lips curved into a thin smile. "Whatever it takes."

"Now, now, let's not be hasty," her father blustered. "I'm sure we can work this out."

"Daddy!" Steffi protested. "I can't believe you're wasting your time with this. Who cares about the underpants? They're talking about getting married."

"Baby, this is important," her father argued.

"No, what *I* want is important. And I do not want Lucie as my sister-in-law!" She bolted out from under her father's arm and skated out the door on her cha-cha heels, not even bothering to wait for Kyle.

As her dad wheeled and ran after Steffi, Ian made frantic gestures at Kyle to go, too. "Be a puppy," he mouthed. "Follow her." As Kyle finally got the idea and took off in pursuit, Ian turned to Lucie. "See? It's working like a charm. Steffi's on the verge of dumping Kyle and your dad is warming up to a compromise on Pandora's Boxers."

"Don't count your chickens—" Lucie started, but then they heard a big thump and a screech from outside.

She ran to the window, where she saw the tail end of Steffi's red convertible speeding away down the lane. In her wake, their father was kneeling next to a prone body.

"Oh, my God! I think she hit Kyle!"

Ian ran outside in a flash, with Lucie on his heels.

"It wasn't her fault," Don Webster insisted. "She spun out and clipped him with her back fender when it swung around. She didn't see him, I'm sure."

But they had no time for that nonsense. As Ian bent down, Kyle made an inarticulate noise, a cry of pure agony. "Kyle?" Ian prompted. "Your eyes are open. Are you okay?"

"I think—I think maybe I broke my leg," Kyle mumbled, grinding his teeth, screwing up his face with pain. "Maybe both of them."

"Don't move," Ian ordered. He turned to Lucie. "Call 911. I think he needs an ambulance."

Lucie made a beeline for the phone. Behind her, she heard Ian say gently, "I was kidding when I told you to break both your legs, Ky. You do know that, right?"

IAN WAS STILL IN A DAZE. His brother was in the hospital with a hairline fracture of his right fibula and a clean fracture of his left tibia—which basically meant two broken legs. On the bright side, he also got a get-out-of-your-honeymoon-free card.

Meanwhile, the Mackintosh parents and little sister were camped out in the waiting room, unwilling to leave until Kyle was assigned to a room. Lucie was there, too—she'd driven him—but she'd taken a chair by herself, over in the corner.

And then there was Steffi, his brand-new sister-in-law, the same one who'd run over his brother, weeping and moaning all over the place, acting like she was in the center of a Greek tragedy. Not that she'd wasted a minute blaming herself or even admitting what she'd done.

"Poor Kyle!" she wailed, leaving wet spots on the shoulder of Ian's dad's jacket. "This is so unfair. Now we'll never get to Hawaii."

"He'll be fine," Ian's father said in a soothing voice. "They're keeping him in the hospital for a few days, but he may even be able to come home on Thursday."

But Steffi kept sobbing and lamenting her fate, utterly inconsolable.

Ian knew what was coming. Any minute now, his mother was going to pat Steffi on the top of her sleek, dark head and suggest that she come home with them and stay as long as she liked, as long as Kyle was recuperating. The words were already forming on his meddling mom's lips.

He paced over to the corner where Lucie sat.

"Okay," he said in an undertone, "now I'm definitely getting my brother out of this marriage. Throwing the wedding gifts out the window was one thing. But mowing him down with her car is going too far."

"Poor Kyle," Lucie murmured. She looked about as depressed as he felt. "Do you think it's our fault? We told him to go after her and act like a puppy. But who knew she'd really run him down like a dog?"

"It's not our fault." He stood up, jamming his hands in his pockets. "But I'm more committed than ever to helping him."

"It's not going to be easy." Lucie inclined her head in the direction of his parents. "I just heard your mom ask if Steffi wanted to move in for the duration. Now that she's found a way to worm her way inside the mother ship, I don't think even flagrant hanky-panky from us is going to do it."

"Damn it. When she bolted out of there, I thought we had her." Ian sat back down. "What was it she said? 'I can't be married to someone whose brother is in love with Lucie.' I really thought she was taking the bait."

Lucie rubbed her eyes. "Yeah, well, trust Steffi to use even a car accident to her own advantage."

"She and your father insist it wasn't her fault, that Kyle walked into the back of her car."

"Yeah, and her cashmere sweater cut itself to ribbons in ninth grade."

He shook his head. "There's got to be something we can do."

"There is." Edging over in the uncomfortable plastic seat, Lucie looked at him with warmth and sympathy in her eyes. "Listen, Ian, I've been thinking. We were fooling around, playing games, having fun. But it's gone far enough. Let's end it."

He felt a pang that had nothing to do with Steffi or Kyle. *Let's end it.* It sounded so cold. And the funny thing was, he didn't want it to end. "And let Steffi win? You've got to be kidding."

"She wouldn't have to win. We both know that if Kyle were to file for divorce immediately, Steffi would automatically look to my dad to tell her what to do," she said softly.

"And he's not going to back down," Ian returned. "I already know that. What I didn't tell you..." He glanced at her, wondering whether it was wise to share this much. Aw, hell, she already knew most of it, anyway. "Lucie, Kyle and I stand to make twenty million dollars off our m-tosh.com. If your father gets wind of that, there will never be a divorce."

"Twenty *million?* That makes this an even better idea." She glanced down at her clasped hands. "I need to do this now, *before* he finds out about the twenty million dollars."

"Do what?"

"You know how threatened he was by what you said, about helping me with Pandora's Boxers. So I can tell him that I'm willing to forget about Pandora's Boxers forever if he can convince Steffi to give Kyle a quick and easy annulment. If I fold, he brokers an annulment. I think he might do it."

"No."

"But there's a chance," Lucie tried. "It would be over and Kyle would be free."

But Ian was adamant. He was not going to trade his brother's freedom for Lucie's dream. Once again rising to his feet, he said firmly, "We'll do both, just the way we agreed. Both."

"But, Ian—"

"No. Not even an issue, Lucie."

"Ian, dear, I hate to interrupt..." His mother stood at his shoulder.

"What is it?"

"They've transferred Kyle to a room, so we're going to go see him right now. And then we'll get out of here and let him get some sleep." She stretched up to kiss her older son on the cheek. "Would you and Lucie like to come back to the house, too?"

"No, Mom, that's okay." He couldn't see bringing Lucie to any house with Steffi in it.

But his mother persisted. "I know you leased out the house that you and Kyle were sharing before he got married, so you've been at loose ends, dear. And it's been very sweet of Lucie to put you up for a few days. But we'd love to have you come home." She paused, and he could swear he saw a devious light in her eye. What was she up to? "Steffi's coming, and since Lucie is her sister..."

"Half sister," Lucie said woodenly.

"Maybe it would be good for Steffi to have family there," his mom added.

Or maybe it would kick Steffi right over the edge if

Lucie horned in, sharing the bosom of Barbie's Dream Family...

"I think we'd like that, Mom. I think Lucie and I would like that very much."

"Excuse me?" Lucie sat up straighter. "What would we like?"

"My mother has just invited us home for a few days, darling. You and I." He caught her hand and brought it to his lips. "Family dinners with Mom, Dad, my sister, Jessica. And, of course, Steffi."

"Family dinners? With Steffi? And me?" Her eyes reflected horror. "Are you sure about this?"

He didn't hold back his wicked grin. "I think it could be just the ticket."

THE MACKINTOSH MANSION was quite spectacular, in a hunting lodge sort of way, all dark paneling and impossibly high ceilings, decorated with needlepoint pillows and tapestry chairs and fresh flowers on exquisite antique tables. When Myra Mackintosh led the way up the stairs and then down a long hall to the guest wing, Lucie had a chance to see more of the posh, elegant house.

"I feel terrible you're toting your own bags, Lucie, dear," Mrs. Mackintosh offered. "But we only keep a few day servants, and no one stays this late. George has already turned in, I'm afraid, and I couldn't find Ian. So I do apologize."

"It's no problem. Really." She hoisted one bag over her shoulder and kept a firm grip on the other one, which held a small portable sewing machine and a few garments she was working on. She didn't want to be bored while she was here, no matter how long the visit lasted.

Craning her neck, she checked the portraits on the walls for any family resemblance, but didn't catch any. They passed several doors in the corridor, but it was all quiet and still, as if none of the rooms were occupied. Finally, Myra Mackintosh pushed open the last door.

"This is my favorite guest room, Lucie, dear. I had it made up for you."

Lucie peeked inside. *Wow.* The room was lovely, with its gleaming mahogany four-poster dripping in luxurious lemon-colored linens, a cozy cushioned window seat, and a bouquet of daisies and yellow roses in a cut-glass vase on the polished secretary.

It was perfect. Except for the fact that Ian's clothes were already strewn across the bed.

With her suitcases in her hands, Lucie stepped back. They had discussed this before she went back to the cottage to pack. She'd told him that this new temporary living arrangement wouldn't change anything with regard to their hands-off policy, and in fact, it might make things easier. After all, she really doubted that either of them would be in the mood for funny stuff with his parents and his little sister hanging around.

Of course, he hadn't said a peep about the fact that none of them would even be in the same wing.

Still, she had no intention of sharing a bedroom or a bed with Ian. There was no point in ignoring the obvious—thirty seconds in that four-poster and the two of them would be all over each other, good intentions, linens and pillows thrown to the four winds.

She averted her eyes. "Mrs. Mackintosh—"

"Please, dear, call me Myra."

"Myra, thank you so much for your wonderful hospitality," Lucie said delicately. "This is a beautiful room. Really. But out of respect for you and your husband, I think I should have a separate room."

"Don't be silly, Lucie," she pooh-poohed, waving a hand in the air. "George and I aren't that old, you know. And I would never keep you and Ian apart when you're so clearly champing at the bit to be together. I'm just thrilled to death you're here."

As she spoke, Ian emerged from the attached powder room, whistling as he toweled off his face.

"Ian," Lucie began in an ominous tone. "Didn't we discuss this, *darling?* Didn't we decide we should have separate rooms?"

He shrugged carelessly, the traitor. "Mom thought that was denying the obvious." He plunked himself down on the bed. "That we're in love, I mean."

"Ian—"

"Now don't argue with me, Lucie," Mrs. Mackintosh said coyly. She backed out of the room, catching the door and starting to close it. "You two settle in and get a good night's sleep. Everyone is going to be running back and forth to the hospital tomorrow, so don't expect to see too much of us. Oh, and Thursday night, Cook's planning a special dinner for us to celebrate— we hope—Kyle getting released, as well as having both of our daughters-in-law under our roof. So plan on that, all right?" And then she was gone.

"Both of our daughters-in-law?" Lucie echoed, dropping her luggage right where she stood. "Ian, this is terrible! She's acting like we're already married, and we're not even engaged. We don't even like each other! How can you do this to your mother?"

He patted the bed, indicating she should join him. "Take it easy, Lu. I don't know what she really thinks or whether she's just messing with our heads. My mother is a complicated woman. Come on over here. Relax."

He'd just called her Lu. That was a new one. She'd never had a nickname in her entire life. Lucie frowned. "She referred to me as her daughter-in-law, Ian. I don't want her thinking that's going to happen. It's not fair to play games with such a nice, trusting person."

"Oh, she'll get over it." He lay back, propping his head on his arms. "I mean, we're not getting married, we're not even really a couple, so she'll have to get over it, won't she?"

"That's what I mean! How can you do that to your own mother?"

"Believe me, I understand her better than you do." Sitting up halfway, he sent her a cynical glance. "She's pleased as punch that I've brought a woman home. She gave up on me ages ago, yet here I am with a reasonable prospect. So she's trying to make sure you don't escape."

"Don't be ridiculous." But Lucie perched on the edge of the bed. "I suppose I should be flattered she thinks I'm a reasonable prospect for her son. But I don't know what to think." As Ian slipped an arm around her, pulling her onto the four-poster with him, she whispered, "Except that this is a terrible idea."

"Oh, come on." His lips found her neck and then her ear. "Do you want my parents and Steffi to think we're not for real?"

"No..."

"Exactly. And if we make a big deal of separate bedrooms, what are they going to think?" He nibbled on her earlobe, brushing kisses inside her collar, loosening the ribbon in her hair.

"But we had a pact," she tried, sinking further into the pillows.

Now his warm, wet mouth moved over her chin, closer to her lips, not quite kissing her the way she craved to be kissed. "We can get back to the pact later," he murmured, sliding his tongue over her bottom lip, making her shiver, angling his body over hers.

"Oh, Ian..." But her hands reached for him, too, encircling his neck, urging him closer.

His mouth covered hers, his tongue plunged inside, and he kissed her savagely, all restless male energy and overwhelming force. There was no denying him, not that she wanted to. As usual, her brain abandoned her and her wildest impulses took over when Ian touched her. She plastered herself against him, she met him thrust for thrust, and she moaned into that unrelenting kiss. They spun over completely, and then again, knocking his clothes off the bed, smashing into each other and the headboard in their reckless haste.

Finally, when they were both panting for breath, Ian pulled back.

As she gulped air back into her lungs, Lucie let her head fall flat against the pillow. How the heck did that happen? How did she let it happen, again and again? "Why do I turn into oatmeal every time you touch me?"

But he whispered, "You don't taste like oatmeal. More like..." He dipped down and licked her collarbone. "More like Paris." He licked her again, only the slope of her neck this time. When he spoke, his words were soft, indistinct, and hypnotic. "Like a misty night in Paris. There we are, you and I, sharing a glass of excellent champagne in the moonlight, on our balcony at the Georges V, and then we slip inside..." his lips brushed hers, ever so gently "...and make love every way we know how, until we pass out from sheer exhaustion."

"Good lord." She sat up far enough to glare at him. "Ian, this is me you're talking to, not some Feather person. I am *so* not misty nights in Paris or champagne and sex until people pass out."

"You are to me," he said simply.

"Well, I'm not to me."

How long ago was it that she'd wished for a man to take her to Paris in the rain and the moonlight? And when had she decided that Ian was not at all that man? It made it seem worse that he had somehow accidentally tapped into—and cheapened—her fantasy. She wanted to smack him.

She shoved her hair out of her face and scrambled off

the side of the bed. "Listen to me, Ian. We're not doing this. This bed or this room, I mean."

He started to protest, but she wasn't waiting for that. "I'm not budging on this one," she told him sternly. "I mean, look at us! How long were we in here before we were rolling around on the bed? A minute? Two?"

"Lucie," he tried, "why not?"

"Oh, no. We agreed—no fooling around. And I don't care what you tell your mother, but one of us is moving to another room." She began to pick up his shirts and pants from the floor, purposefully tossing them back near his duffel bag. "Probably you, because I really like this one."

His blue eyes were hooded as his gaze raked her. "Okay, okay. You can stay here. My old room is actually next door, and it's empty, so I can probably sneak back in there as long as we don't tell her."

"Good." She didn't want to be so mean or inflexible, but a person had to protect herself, didn't she? All this good-natured romping around was nothing to him, but to her...

Well, it was all quite earth-shattering. She raised a weak hand to her forehead. She'd never felt like this before, like if she didn't have her hands and her mouth on him in the next three seconds, she'd die. Like she wanted to strip him naked, tie him to the four-poster, and play naughty games all day and all night. Like she really wanted to run off to Paris and start guzzling champagne on the balconies of luxury hotels.

"I am losing my mind," she said slowly.

"I said I'd move next door." He grabbed a pair of

pants and a dress shirt off the pile on the floor. "But be discreet, will you? We still want them all to think we're sharing."

"I won't tell anyone if you won't."

Ian shook his head, sending Lucie a cynical glare. "I can't believe I'm sneaking *out* of my girlfriend's room instead of into it."

"I'm not your girlfriend," she called after him as he checked the hallway and then slipped out like some sort of cat burglar.

With him gone—thank goodness—Lucie stalked into the expansive private bath opening off the bedroom, closed the door quietly behind her, and then slumped against the back of it.

"Aieee!" she screamed, hoping the bathroom was well sound-proofed.

And to think, she'd actually predicted his parents' house would be an improvement over her too-small, too-intimate cottage.

8

WHAT WITH EVERYONE spending so much time at the
hospital and on the road back and forth to the hospital,
Lucie's first day at the Mackintosh mansion was actually very uneventful. She almost ran into Steffi in the
breakfast room, but her half sister stuck her nose in the
air and left in a huff, so there weren't any fistfights or
anything.

Lucie and Ian stopped by to play cards with Kyle
later in the day, and they all had fun, even if she did
cheat shamelessly so that Kyle could win. What else
could she do? He had two broken legs and he was still
married to Steffi. It wasn't like he hadn't been pun-
ished enough already.

Other than that, with the members of the household
in and out and far too occupied to pry, Lucie found it a
major relief to have one day where she wasn't involved
in pretense, intrigue or any kind of intimate game with
Ian. And as for him...

He'd apparently decided to play the Boy Scout for
the time being. Thank goodness. With him ruffling her
nerves and rousing her senses, she simply couldn't
think. But all he did was send her these enigmatic
glances and slip quietly away if there was any danger

of them being left alone together. It was a bit disconcerting, but better than the alternative.

She actually caught his gaze once or twice and did *not* think about him in or out of skimpy underwear, and that was a major improvement.

In fact, things were perfectly calm until Thursday evening, when the "special dinner" loomed on the horizon. Lucie was a little anxious, since she didn't know exactly what to wear, but Ian told her she could put on a pair of Pandora's Boxers PJs for all he cared and she would still be just fine. While she appreciated the sentiment, that still didn't tell her what to wear.

She finally settled on the most sedate thing she had—a pale pink sweater and a floaty silk skirt with swirls of pink and rose dappled across it. She threw on about six small beaded bracelets and a pair of antique pearl drop earrings, and decided that was as good as it got.

"You look lovely," Mr. Mackintosh commented, kissing her on the cheek as she entered the dining room.

"Thank you so much."

He seemed genuinely happy to see her. And yet she felt awful. A simple compliment from Ian's father and she was consumed with guilt. *They are so kind and gracious, and yet it's all a lie. Ian, how can we do this?*

But he wasn't there to ask.

Surveying the long room, she saw that the table was set beautifully with gleaming china, silver candlesticks, and crystal goblets. Mrs. Mackintosh and Jessica stood stiffly near the windows on the opposite side, while Steffi, elegant in a severe, sleeveless red linen dress and major diamond earrings, held court at the end of the table. She looked seriously cranky.

"Where's Ian?" Lucie asked with concern. "He came down ages ago."

"He went to break Kyle out of the slammer," George Mackintosh teased.

"Seriously, dear, Kyle's been released, so Ian went to pick him up." Mrs. Mackintosh smiled. "Ian insisted. It's the way it's always been with those two—Kyle gets into a scrape and Ian gets him out. We're holding back dinner until they arrive. I hope you don't mind."

"Mind? I'm thrilled. I'm so glad Kyle gets to come home." She glanced at Steffi, who still had a sour, unpleasant expression on her face. "Steffi? Isn't that terrific?"

"Hmph." Slugging back a big swallow of wine, Steffi muttered, "I don't see why we can't go ahead and eat. I thought this dinner was in *my* honor, after all."

"It's a celebration for Kyle, to be out of the hospital, and to say welcome to *both* you and Lucie," Myra Mackintosh said with a definite edge of reprimand.

Lucie held her breath. Steffi wasn't going to like that. At home, she'd have knocked over her wineglass, sworn at the maid, and demanded to be brought food immediately on a silver platter while Lucie was sent to the kitchen. But apparently she had the good sense to contain the worst of her bad habits now that she was in someone else's house.

"I'm waiting, aren't I?" she asked petulantly, scraping lines in the heavy tablecloth with the tines of her fork.

Mrs. Mackintosh frowned and made a point of looking in the other direction. Unable to miss the chill in the room, Lucie hovered near the doorway, not ready to sit if Steffi was going to keep sulking down there and annoying everyone.

"So, Lucie, Ian tells us that you design lingerie," George Mackintosh said briskly. "Sounds fascinating."

"He did?"

There was a huge, aggrieved sigh from Steffi's end of the table, but the others all smiled encouragingly.

"It sounds really cool, Lucie," Jessica said shyly. All of sixteen, she couldn't be interested in lingerie yet, could she? Well, maybe.

"Ian really told you about this?" All three Mackintoshes nodded, so Lucie continued. "My mother started a company, Pandora's Boxers, that was quite successful in the late '70s. Perhaps you remember it?"

Myra nodded. "Oh, yes. They had beautiful things. I wondered whatever happened to that label."

"I'm trying to relaunch it," Lucie explained, gaining enthusiasm, "branching out from just ladies' lingerie to men's undergarments as well."

"Yes," Ian's mother said quickly. "Ian told us about some of your designs." There was a twinkle of mischief in her eyes, making them look very much like her son's.

"He did?" She couldn't believe he would've spilled any details on that score.

"Mmm-hmm." The older woman moved closer. "I

understand he wants to help with your relaunch. Ian said you'll be selling your lingerie on the Internet but need more focus on marketing. Have I got that right, dear?"

That was the first Lucie'd heard of any of this. So Ian was serious about being part of the Pandora's Boxers team?

"I thought that was so generous of you, dear, to share your business plans with Ian. Since he and Kyle decided to sell that..." She frowned. "What is it called, George? Dot-something? Anyway, with that off their plates, I know they'll need new projects. Though goodness knows they won't need any more money. But Kyle now has Steffi, and Ian has you and your boxers, and I think that's just delightful. Like a hobby for him."

"Thank you. I'm grateful he wants to help." Astonished was more like it. Lucie ventured a glance Steffi's way, to see if she'd picked up the clue about the dotcom that yielded so much money, but Steffi seemed too interested in emptying her wineglass to care. "I know how successful Ian has been. To have someone like him willing to help me, well, I'm amazingly lucky," Lucie said with all honesty.

"Lucie?" Jessica asked, slipping around to her other side. "Have you ever designed any clothes for kids? Like, my age?"

"Um, no. No, I haven't."

"Because that would be awesome. Camis and boxer shorts, I mean. Or tiny tanks and matching lounge pants." The teenager smiled eagerly. "It might be something to consider."

"You're absolutely right, Jessica. Why not?" Lucie tipped her head to the side. "I mean, all my stuff so far has been for fuller figures. But why not go for smaller ones, too?"

"Exactly."

"I have some things up in my room that I'm working on," Lucie noted. "I could bring some down and show you later, if you're interested. In the women's area, I've been moving away from bras and panties and working more into lounging clothes. Like things you can wear for yoga. I'm sort of itching to design my own."

"Cool!" Jessica enthused. "I take yoga three times a week. I love yoga!"

"Now I'll *have* to show you what I came up with and see what you think. You can be my consultant. Because I think the fabric that you use is so important—"

She was interrupted by a rather hearty call from out in the front hall. "Hey, we're here," Ian shouted. "Anyone waiting for us?"

There was poor Kyle on crutches, with Ian helping, and the rest of the family beaming as they ran out to greet them and pull them into the dining room. They were all so happy, exuding such warmth and joy, that the scene resembled something out of Dickens. Of course, in this version, Tiny Tim was six feet tall, with casts up to the knee on both legs, and the Cratchits lived in a mansion. Still, the sentiment was there.

Meanwhile, Steffi was conspicuously uninvolved. She managed to wave from the end of the table and murmur, "Hello, Kyle," but no one really noticed.

"How can you be on crutches with casts on both legs?" Mrs. Mackintosh asked with a gasp.

"It's a walking cast on my right leg. The fracture was small enough I can put some weight on it." Kyle winced, pushing out his crutches as he fell into a chair. "I am so happy to be home."

"And we are so happy to have you here, dear." His mother kissed him and fussed over him until her husband told her she had to go sit down or they would never get dinner.

And then, finally, the soup was served. Dishes came and went—a cucumber salad and poached salmon and new peas and potatoes—and everyone seemed to be talking at once, with lots more questions about Lucie's lingerie and Kyle's prognosis. Jessica started flipping peas across the table at Ian, which started gales of laughter as he retaliated with rolls.

And Steffi pouted through it all, all the way to the scrumptious watermelon-mango sorbet.

Raising her voice, she demanded, "Are you going to be ignoring me all night? I'm your guest. This is so rude I can't stand it!"

The silence was deafening.

As Lucie considered apologizing on behalf of the Webster family, Mrs. Mackintosh said politely, "I'm sorry you're not enjoying yourself, Steffi. Perhaps we do seem boisterous to outsiders. I hope you'll forgive our high spirits just this once."

But Ian muttered, "I think we know who the rude one is."

No one said anything at first, until Jessica giggled

and neatly pitched a mint leaf garnish from the sorbet into her brother's water glass. Then the ruckus began again, Kyle entered the fray, and Lucie passed her own mint leaves to Jessica for ammunition.

At that point, Steffi shoved herself away from the table and stomped out of the dining room.

When Steffi was well out of earshot, Myra Mackintosh leaned over to speak to her younger son. "Kyle," she said plainly, "I don't know what we did wrong when we raised you. But whatever it was, I don't think it was bad enough to justify you marrying that girl."

"I think we can get him out of it, Mom." Ian smiled with satisfaction. "Who knows? After this, maybe she'll leave on her own."

"I tried to be nice to her for your sake, Kyle. Really I did." The Mackintosh matron shook her head. "But it was a losing battle." Her husband and daughter murmured their agreement.

As Lucie watched, surprised that they were so open about their disdain for Steffi. Then the Mackintoshes raised their glasses.

"To Kyle. Welcome home!" Jessica toasted.

"Here's to Steffi's speedy departure," Kyle declared. "I was temporarily insane, but I've regained my sanity, and I want to thank you all for bearing with me during the duration."

"And to Lucie," Myra offered, "a charming and lovely girl who couldn't be less like her sister."

"Half sister," Ian and Lucie chorused.

With a sense of wistful awe, Lucie watched them laugh and smile and poke fun at each other. In her life, the concept of family, at its best, had meant a marvelously eccentric mother who often forgot dinner but let her eat popcorn and watch *The Three Stooges* instead of going to bed. At its worst, it had meant chilly distance and disapproval.

But never anything like this. They were so at ease with each other, so relaxed and happy. No, Miss Manners would probably not approve of the food fight. But Lucie loved its spontaneity and charm. In short, she thought this family was wonderful.

If only she got to keep them.

Don't get too attached, Lucie. They're not yours. You just get them on loan.

But the least she could do was enjoy them while she had them, right? She lifted her own wineglass and cleared her throat. "Excuse me?"

"Shh, it's Lucie's turn," Ian ordered.

"First," she announced, "I would like to propose a toast to all of you for being so kind to an outsider—"

That spurred a flurry of protests, but she held up her hand to forestall them. "I'm not finished. Okay, so first, to all of you, and then, to Ian, who brought me into your midst."

Goodwill and sentiment swamped her as she gazed at him. She could only hope that her emotions didn't radiate from her face, flooding him, scaring him to death. She knew him well enough to know that he wouldn't know what to do with the tenderness and joy she felt in her heart at that moment. But she couldn't keep herself from feeling what she was feeling, could she?

Her lips curved into a soft smile. "To Ian."

He didn't exactly smile back, but she read heat and a certain anticipation in his eyes.

"I think Kyle is tired," his mother said suddenly. But she wasn't looking at Kyle. No, her eyes were fixed on Ian and Lucie and the smoldering glances passing back and forth between them. "It's late. Let's call it a night, shall we?"

"Mom, I'm not ready for bed," Jessica objected.

"Yes, you are. Come on, Jess, help your father and me get Kyle to his room. Here are your crutches, sweetheart. I've put you in the first floor guest room, the one where Aunt Sylvia always used to stay. And don't worry, your bride is all the way on the other side of the house..."

As easily as that, they cleared the dining room, which left Ian and Lucie very much alone.

Casually, he took her hand and led her up the stairs. It wasn't until they were halfway down their own hallway that Lucie put the brakes on.

"Ian," she entreated, dragging her heels, "I know where this is going, and I still don't think—"

"What? That we should share a room?" His grin was crooked and adorable as he caught her by the waist and spun her around in the middle of the corridor, sending her skirt billowing. "I think it should be crystal clear by now that we don't need a bedroom or a bed to get into trouble."

And then he tickled her. "Hey!" She giggled, swatting at his hands. "Ian, stop it."

It only took a few seconds for him to capture both of

her hands in one of his, to back her up against the wall with her hands held high above her head, and to keep up the tickling assault until she could barely stand.

"This isn't fair," she protested. But he didn't seem to care. She was past laughter and into hiccups now. "I'm still not sleeping with you. I don't care if you keep this up for hours—you still have to go to your own room and I'll go to mine."

His fingers grew more gentle, and he switched to kisses, barely brushing his lips over her cheeks and the tip of her nose. One hand still clasped both of hers out of the way, but his free hand crept under her sweater, under the soft, stretchy fabric of her bra, sliding it out of the way, cupping and teasing her breast until her nipple peaked hard into his palm.

Oh, he was good at this.

"Ian..."

"Who says I have sleeping in mind?" he whispered, blowing into her ear, making her shiver. "Who says I don't want to make love to you right here in the hallway?"

"You can't."

"Oh, yes," he said roughly, "I can."

He shoved her against the wall, greedily finding her mouth, releasing her hands as he lifted her off the floor. She didn't mean to kiss him back. She didn't mean to tangle her arms and legs around him. But she did.

Somehow her skirt ended up bunched around her waist as her bare thighs rode his hips. She ripped his shirt open and he pushed her sweater up over her arms, casting it away, exposing her full, round breasts to his hungry eyes.

"Fabulous," he murmured, in this low, thick voice that undid her.

Trapped between him and the wall, with his skin pressed to hers, torso to torso, hip to hip, she already skated on the edge of incredible, intoxicating pleasure. But...

"Wait, wait." Gasping for breath, she bracketed his face with her hands, searching his eyes. "We can't...in the hallway, I mean. What if someone comes?"

"We're the only people up here." His voice was low and unsteady as he assured her, "My parents' room is on the other side of the house. Kyle and Jessie are downstairs. We're all alone up here."

"Okay."

And his mouth covered hers once more. His hands peeled her panties down, squeezed her bottom, urged her nearer, rocked her into a rhythm she couldn't deny. *Oh, lord.* They were actually going to do this in the hallway. She had never felt so turned on in her life. She twisted to reach for his belt, scrambling for the buckle, dying to get this moving, to fulfill her mounting need.

As his trousers pooled around his ankles, Lucie moaned, hooking one leg behind him, rubbing up and down against him. She was so wet and so ready and they had barely begun.

"Stop." He stiffened. His hand slashed across her mouth, keeping her still. "Did you hear that?"

She didn't hear anything but her own heartbeat. Or was that his?

But he held her there, smashed into the wall, as he listened. And then she heard it, too. Voices. Low, intense voices, coming up the stairs and heading for this hallway.

Her eyes met his. What now? She was still dizzy with desire and in no condition to either get her clothes back together or crawl twenty feet down the hall into the bedroom. And yet they could hardly stay where they were.

The voices grew louder.

Just as she began to hyperventilate, Ian wrapped his arms tightly around her and hurled both of them inside the nearest door. A linen closet.

It was large as linen closets went, but barely big enough for two people. She was still stuck to his body, still excited and trembling, as he dumped her onto a shelf full of sheets, spun around, ducked far enough into the hall to grab his pants and her sweater, and come careening back in.

Quickly, he pulled Lucie back into his arms. He kissed her hard and fast and then held her there, secure in his embrace. She had no idea if this was a protective gesture, in case someone opened the closet door, or if he was just too far gone to rein in his libido completely.

Breathing heavily, trying to get herself under control, Lucie could make out two voices now. And one of them was Steffi's.

Her fear of discovery, and her curiosity over what Steffi was doing here and with whom, mixed together in a crazy way, heightening the adrenaline and desire still sizzling in her veins. She wiggled against Ian, just a little, enjoying the idea that *she* could torture *him* for once, and that he couldn't act on it while they were stuck in this place. By the way his eyes narrowed and his heartbeat quickened next to hers, she knew he understood the dangerous game she was playing.

Outside their closet, Steffi claimed, "There's nobody up here. Just an empty hallway and you and me."

"Oh, baby," the man returned hotly, in a nasal, almost whiny voice. Definitely not Kyle. "Wanna do it right here?"

And Lucie heard slushy, smacky noises that could only mean one thing. Steffi and her boyfriend were making out in the hall.

She swallowed. Ian's hands framed her face, pushing into her hair. Gently, he slid his mouth over hers. She closed her eyes...tasted his tongue.... She savored every second of it, the goings-on outside the closet briefly fading from her thoughts.

Inches away, Steffi suddenly moaned, "Oh, Paolo, I want you, big boy."

Paolo? Big boy? She couldn't help it. A giggle bubbled up.

Ian's hand immediately covered her mouth, but Steffi said, "I thought I heard something."

"Naaah. It was nuthin'. Just a creak or somethin'. You know old houses."

"Oh, Paolo," Steffi panted, "I want you now, but not here, not in the hallway."

Lucie closed her eyes, pleading with whomever might be listening to the prayers of bad girls. *Please don't let them pick the closet, too.*

But Steffi whispered, "Let's go outside, back to the garden, where we did it before." In a flirty, little-girl voice, she inquired, "You liked it there, didn't you, big boy?"

"The bench in the garden shed?" Her lover's voice sounded perplexed, definitely whiny now. "I thought you said you got a splinter."

"No, no," Steffi snapped. "I meant the gazebo. It's dark. No one will see us."

The mysterious Paolo chuckled. There was a muffled thump against the wall and then another, followed by an audible groan.

Lovemaking noises outside, lovemaking inside... What was it about this hall?

The closet was hot and the air was close and perspiration trickled down her cleavage. But it was nothing like the heat raging inside her. Ian had one hand over her mouth and the other on her breast, tweaking her nipple, pinching her and quite deliberately plaguing her until she wanted to scream with frustration. She felt like sliding down his body and melting into a puddle on the floor of the linen closet. If her damn half sister and her horny beau didn't vacate this hallway within the next five seconds, Lucie swore she was going to climb on top of Ian and take him, anyway.

Footsteps. She held herself rigid, listening. They were leaving. Thank God, they were leaving.

As the voices and footsteps subsided, Lucie let out a long breath. She grabbed Ian at the precise moment he grabbed her, pushing the last scraps of their clothes out of the way. He pressed her back into the shelf, kissing her, caressing her, as she wrapped her legs around him.

When he plunged inside, hard and hot and wonderful, so full and so welcome, Lucie met him stroke for stroke, crying out her immense relief, her escalating pleasure.

Already. Already it was building and pulsing, pushing her higher.

She remembered now. She remembered how fast and hard she came the first time and the second...

But she'd have to think about that later. Right now, all she could take in was Ian and his flesh next to her flesh, his strong, long body ramming her into the wall, into a quivering, shattering climax neither one of them could contain.

It was mindless. It was marvelous.

And she wanted more.

HE COULDN'T BELIEVE he'd just made love to Lucie in a closet.

Towels, sheets and pillowcases had toppled from the shelves and spilled to the floor and they hadn't even noticed. His mind had been on one single thing—to make love to Lucie, rough and fast, to take her somewhere neither of them had ever been.

To be honest, it wasn't making love. It was lust, pure and simple. Good old, healthy lust. Two people pushed beyond endurance by the combined force of their own frustration.

That was his story and he was sticking to it.

"Are you okay?" he whispered, pulling back far

enough to survey the damage. He didn't know why he was bothering to keep his voice down now, after he'd growled her name and she'd shouted his. Not to mention the fact that they'd pounded into the wall loud enough to wake the dead. Thank goodness everybody else slept on the other side of the house.

As he gave her a quick once-over, he saw that Lucie's face was flushed and her mouth a little puffy from relentless kisses, but otherwise she looked none the worse for wear, much to his relief.

This conflagration between them, this bonfire in the linen closet, was exactly what he'd wanted for days. So why was he shaking in his boots, afraid he'd hurt her feelings or bruised her pretty little bottom as well as her pride?

"Lucie?" he said again, carefully scanning as much pale skin as he could make out in the dim closet. "Are you sure you're okay?"

"I'm fine." She smiled lazily, stretching and yawning. "Could we try this again, maybe take a little more time, maybe somewhere a little more comfortable?"

He sagged with relief. She really was fine. She didn't hate him. Better yet, she wanted to do it again.

Suddenly full of energy, he slid open the door enough to check the hallway. "All clear," he said out loud. "Let's go."

With her hand in his, scooping up their various bits of clothing, he darted out of the closet and back towards Lucie's room, feeling as euphoric as a five-year-old playing tag on the playground.

Inside the yellow room, Ian dived under the covers

while Lucie took a quick shower. The minute he hit the bed, he realized how exhausted he was. Maybe a nap would be a good idea before they started round two.

But the sound of her shower sputtered out, and Lucie strolled out of the bathroom wearing a towel on her head and a pair of shortie pajamas with puffy clouds scattered across them. Either she had sleep on her agenda or she was into getting her clothes ripped off again. How intriguing that she was just as sexy in cotton PJs, scrubbed clean, with wet hair.

"Ian, while we were in the closet..."

"Yes?" he murmured, wondering where this was going, not sure he wanted to know. He remembered now why he made a habit of not fooling around with complicated women. They had a tendency to overthink everything.

Lucie knelt on the bed. "When we were in the closet, who in the world did we hear in the hall?"

Not what he expected. A lot less intense than it could've been if Lucie had been experiencing second thoughts in the shower. *Phew.* "Well, I'd say it was Steffi, for sure. And some guy named Paolo." He shrugged. "Do you know anyone named Paolo?"

"I don't think so." She chewed her lip. "But I could swear I've heard that voice before. Kind of gritty, wasn't it? And nasal?"

"Who cares?" he murmured huskily, drawing her hand into his, trying his level best to tip her over on top of him.

He unwound the towel from her hair, flipping back the covers to invite her in. After all, they had all the time in the world, and he wanted to test out a theory. Could they do this soft and slow? How long would they last if they took their time to *make love*, and didn't get caught up in the mad rush of lust?

"Let's worry about Steffi later," he breathed. "Who knows? Maybe by the time we get up, she'll be gone. But right now, this four-poster has our names written all over it."

MORNING LIGHT DRIFTED slowly into the room, casting a soft, warm glow on Lucie.

She opened one eye. "Mmmph," she mumbled, unable to recognize the fuzzy shapes in front of her.

Stretching out an arm, yawning, she blinked, then opened both eyes. A draft tickled her skin, making her quite certain she wasn't wearing a top. Or a bottom.

Naked. In a high, soft bed she vaguely recognized, with intricately carved posts and beautiful, lemon-colored linens bunched around her.

She could hear steady, regular breathing in the bed. Not only that, but she could feel hot puffs of air ruffling her hair, as if someone were lying there, his head just behind hers, breathing on her.

Ian.

"Déjà vu all over again," she whispered, clutching the crocheted edge of the sheet to her front.

"G'morning, Lu," Ian said drowsily. Draping an arm around her shoulder, snuggling closer, he felt warm and cozy, all heated skin and delicious masculine angles.

But Lucie eluded his grasp. She sat up, slipped into

her robe, and tied it tight. What in the world had happened to her hair? She peered at a Medusa-like strand.

"Why is it I completely lose my mind around you?" she inquired, not really expecting an answer. "We weren't going to do this again. You're not my type. I'm not your type. This isn't going anywhere. I realize we were celebrating... What were we celebrating, anyway?"

Ian's eyes were hooded as he lifted his head far enough to gaze at her. "Do we have to do this again?" he asked with exasperation. "How many times have we had this conversation? We're good together, Lucie, over-the-top good. How often does that come along?"

For me? Never.

"So why not stop worrying about where it's going long enough to ask yourself why it has to?" he ventured. "Why aren't we entitled to a careless, no-strings fling like anybody else?"

Lucie kept her mouth shut. She had plenty of thoughts shooting around her brain, but none fit for company.

What if it's not careless or no strings, not on my side of the bed? What if I fell in love with you somewhere in between the kilts and the condoms and the watermelon-mango sorbet?

But there was no way she was sharing even an inkling of that with Ian.

"But what about...? Oh, never mind."

"What about what?" he repeated. She could tell he was trying to be patient and it wasn't working.

"What about last night, in the closet, and after the closet?" Lucie's gaze flickered up to meet his. She could feel warm color flushing her face. "Before, I mean, when we were at the Inn, remember all those condoms?"

"Who could forget?" he asked mockingly.

"Well, this time, in the closet, we were in a rush and we didn't..." She frowned, speeding up. "We didn't use any protection, Ian."

"I know. And we were stupid. We're old enough to know better." He rose partially, leaning on one elbow. "In case you're worried...I know you think I sleep around, but I really don't, and anyway, I swear, Lucie, I have a clean bill of—"

"That's okay." She raised a hand. "I believe you. And I'm healthy, too. I mean, I never do this, so I'm safe." Heavens, this was embarrassing. "But there are other things to consider..."

"Oh." She saw comprehension dawn in his eyes. "Oh!"

Way to go, Lucie. Way to panic a commitment-phobe. Bring up babies, for goodness sake.

"You know," he said after a moment, "I could kind of get into that. And it would make my mom delirious. So, if it turns out that we, well, need to, we could just get married."

"What?"

Her mouth dropped open. How could he be so freaking casual about this, as if he spouted marriage proposals every day? Was she mistaken, or was he the one who thought marriage was for idiots? And why couldn't he behave the way she expected him to for at least five minutes?

She sat back down with a thud. "No, we couldn't."

"Why not?" He slid out of the bed on the other side, pulling on his pants. "Are you just being negative to be negative, or is it me?"

"Neither." She yanked on the ties holding her robe closed, knotting and unknotting them. "I just... I know you think I'm this, thirty-year-old walking biological clock, so you probably think your half-baked proposal is like music to my poor spinster ears, but you're wrong, okay?"

"I never said any of that."

"Yes," she said firmly, "you did."

"Lucie—"

"No, I'm serious. I am not in the market." She shook her head. "I have things I want to do first—"

"Like Pandora's Boxers. I know that."

"Not just that." Lucie fixed her gaze on him, desperate to make her point. "I want to go to Paris, in the rain, and drink champagne and read sonnets and—"

His eyes narrowed. "Then why did you get mad at me when I said something like that?"

"Because you... Because I... Because I don't want you appropriating my romantic fantasies and turning them into cheap sex!" There, she'd said it. And Ian looked totally mystified.

"I hate complicated women," he muttered.

"I'm not that complicated! I just don't fit your stereotype, that's all."

"Listen, I gotta go. I'll see you downstairs." He grabbed the rest of his clothes and made for the door.

Before ducking out, he turned back. "Guess I'd better pick up some condoms, huh?"

Lucie pitched a pillow at him, but it was too late. Her missile hit the door with a useless thump and then fell to the floor.

"He's impossible!" she declared. "Why would I want to marry *him*?"

9

LUCIE HOVERED outside the doors to the morning room with a serious case of trepidation. What could she say to Ian after the disgraceful way she'd behaved? The poor man probably thought he was being a stand-up guy, offering to do the right thing if the need should arise, and she'd retaliated with anger and recriminations. *Jump through the right hoops, Ian, or I'll never allow you to sacrifice your principles and humiliate yourself by marrying me.*

The whole thing was depressing. Not to mention silly, since she never should've brought it up in the first place without some suspicion that it might actually be a problem. "I was just trying to raise the issue of how rash and short-sighted we were being," she said out loud. Talk about a big, fat, ugly backfire.

Still, she wouldn't have been quite so angry if he hadn't added that parting shot about going out for condoms, as if to underline the fact that she was putty in his hands, whenever and wherever he wanted. Even in the linen closet!

But then, she supposed she didn't have to call his marriage proposal half-baked, either. Even though it was.

"What am I going to do about him?" she said under

her breath, pushing open the doors. "What am I going to do about *me?*"

Luckily, she didn't have to decide right now, since Ian wasn't present in the morning room.

Unluckily, Steffi was.

Her half sister was poking at a plate piled with muffins and fruit. "Oh, it's you," she said in her usual snotty tone, and went back to slathering butter on a muffin.

"Why, Steffi, what a surprise." Lucie crossed her arms over her chest. "I thought maybe you'd left after dinner last night. You seemed unhappy."

"I'm fine," she returned with a smug smile. "It takes more than a few rude people to make me turn my back on my wedding vows."

"Uh-huh."

"What did you say?"

"Nothing." Lucie was dying to wipe that smile off Steffi's pointy little face. All she had to do was mention Paolo and the gazebo to make her point about how little it took to distract Steffi from her vows. But Lucie didn't want to blow the whole thing by letting Steffi know too early that her secret was out.

"Why are you lurking in the doorway?" Steffi demanded.

"I just decided I didn't want breakfast after all."

Lucie backed out of there on the double. She had to see Ian. She had to see Ian *now*.

SHE DIDN'T KNOW how she knew, but she did. He would be waiting for her in the library.

A good choice since the library was the last place Steffi would turn up.

There he was, lounging in a chintz wing chair in front of high, crowded bookshelves. Looking about as handsome as anybody had a right to, he had a newspaper propped in front of him. Reading the newspaper, hmm? Or pretending to. Once again, he was only on the front page.

"Ian?" Lucie crept into the library, leaving a good ten feet between her and the wing chair.

His dark brows lowered. The newspaper didn't.

"Okay, before you get any crankier, I'm not here to talk about this morning." She waved her hands to indicate a major change of subject. "The thing is, Steffi's still here. And she doesn't seem in any hurry to leave."

"I know. I saw her."

Hastily, Lucie asked, "You didn't say anything about last night, did you?"

"About her and Paolo, you mean?" Ian discarded his newspaper onto the piecrust table beside him. "I didn't want to show my hand. And I sure don't want to tell Kyle unless I have to."

"Exactly." She paused. "So what are we going to do about her?"

"We've got her dead to rights on the Paolo thing," Ian noted. "It's just a matter of what we do with it."

"I know. I thought that, too." She began to pace in front of him. "But the problem is it's all so sordid. Are we really going to tell people we were making love in a closet and we overheard her boinking some guy named Paolo in the hallway?"

"Uh, probably not."

"Paolo," she repeated. "Wait. I *do* know who that is. Delilah's busboy! How many Paolos with whiny voices can there be?" Her eyes widened. "Steffi is boinking one of the busboys from her own wedding?"

"Jeez, that's tacky." Ian let out a long breath. "That ought to be good enough for a divorce in anybody's book."

Lucie shook her head as she commented darkly, "Yeah, but we need proof. All we know is what we think we heard from the closet."

"I have a feeling," Ian mused, "if we hang around the gazebo long enough we'll trip over them." He indicated a thumb toward the French doors that opened to the gardens. "What do you say? Are you up for a little private investigating? Say, tonight?"

Lucie rubbed her hands together, already imagining the scenario. "We can wear all black, like they do on TV, and bring a video camera and one of those big microphones."

"This isn't *Sixty Minutes.*"

"Oh, come on, Ian." She smiled. "It'll be fun!"

BLACK CLOTHES weren't hard to come by, but the infrared binoculars and video camera were a little trickier. Still, Ian knew people who knew people, and when the clock chimed midnight, they were ready to go. Ian had even drawn a map of the grounds and sketched their path with X's and O's.

"Have you seen Steffi recently?" he asked.

"She didn't come down for dinner, just had a tray in

her room," Lucie told him. "I checked. But I did catch her whispering on the phone this afternoon. Plus she's not in her room now. I checked that, too."

"She didn't go far. Her red convertible is in the garage. *I* checked that," he added.

"So I think she must be running around somewhere on the grounds with Paolo." Lucie's lips tilted up into a wide smile. "And we know it won't be the garden shed."

She wasn't exactly sure why she was enjoying this so much. When they'd discussed how they might help break up Steffi and Kyle's marriage, she hadn't imagined it would involve skullduggery or midnight eavesdropping excursions. And she certainly had no career aspirations to be a spy. But the black clothes, the looming darkness outside the French doors, and even the electronic equipment gave their mission a certain panache.

"Should we synchronize our watches?" she inquired brightly.

One of Ian's dark eyebrows arched. "Don't get too caught up in this. We're sticking together, so no, we don't even need watches. All we have to do is sneak out as close as we can to the gazebo, be very, very quiet and very, very quick, and she and Paolo will never even know we were there."

"Okay, okay. Party pooper."

"This way," he directed, sliding open the French doors and ushering her through. "Stay along the line of hedges until we get to the reflecting pond. There's a statue there and a marble bench. We'll cut across there so we can come up behind the gazebo."

He took her hand and led the way, tiptoeing like the Pink Panther or something, and Lucie had to stop herself from grinning ear to ear. It was just funny, that was all.

"Wait," she whispered. "Did you hear that?"

"No. What?"

"A soft plop. Like something hit the ground. There." She squinted into the dark night, lit only by a crescent moon that peeked through the clouds occasionally and a line of lanterns marking the high stone wall. The lanterns, bobbing in the slight breeze, signaled the boundary of the Mackintosh estate. "I saw a shadow, too," she said softly, her words barely audible. "Over there. I think Paolo just came over the wall."

Ian nodded, bending lower as he skulked around a clump of rose bushes. But his hand was still securely holding hers, carefully, unerringly guiding her along the winding path.

But then he halted suddenly, right in front of her, and Lucie knocked into him before she could stop. She made a small "oof" but caught herself immediately.

Ian held her steady. He mouthed something like, "There," and stabbed his finger in the air to indicate that Steffi and her pal were here, not in the gazebo at all, but right under their noses. A few more steps and they would've been out in the open near the reflecting pool, almost stumbling over the illicit lovers.

Concentrating, Lucie could hear moans and kissing

noises, even from here. Not hard to figure out what they were doing.

Lucie couldn't help it; she had to look. Peering around Ian's shoulder, she put the binoculars to her eyes. Zeroing in, her glasses showed her dark hair and tanned skin—a lot of extremely naked skin—sharply defined against a white marble bench.

"Eeeuw," she muttered. That was a little *too* up close and personal. For the first time, now that it was too late, she realized what that clandestine pursuit might actually turn up. Not just proof, but in-your-face, no-possible-denials smut. "They're doing it on the bench. Wouldn't you think they'd get mosquito bites or something? Eeeuw."

Well, it was no worse than a closet, was it? Except a lot more public.

She made a few gestures of her own, trying to ask Ian if he could get them in focus from this vantage point. He nodded, bringing the small video camera up to his face, whirring off some quick footage.

But he frowned. "Stay here," he whispered, and he circled around to the other side, apparently trying to get a better angle. Lucie chewed on a fingernail to occupy herself, sticking to the spot, staying away from the binoculars. The last thing she needed to see was any more details of her half sister *in flagrante delicto*.

Guess you should've thought of that before you came after her, she told herself. *I didn't know!* she argued back. *I thought they'd be kissing or maybe groping a little. But not all out Erotic Olympics under a lighted statue on a marble bench!*

Meanwhile, what was taking Ian so long? Surely he had enough film of the happy couple by now.

Lucie jiggled her foot and bit her thumbnail. Where was he? Did he fall in the reflecting pool or what?

But a mourning dove cooed right next to her ear and she jumped. She displaced a few twigs, making a small rustle that sounded gigantic in her own ears.

She didn't move.

Suddenly, Ian was behind her, carrying the camera. "Come on. Quick," he whispered. "They're finished. And I think they're coming this way."

"What?"

"I mean it!" a high-pitched voice cried impetuously. "It's over! I mean it, Paolo. Go back out the way you came, and don't ever come back!"

Steffi. And the scraping and lurching noises indicated she had abandoned Paolo and their bench and was tromping this way.

Should they leap into the shrubbery? Confront her? What?

Ian stuck the camera behind Lucie's bottom, pushed her up against the nearest tree, and started to kiss her.

"Oh, my god!" Steffi yelled, slamming to a stop. "Here you are again, all over each other. A person comes out to..." She stopped. "I come out for midnight bird watching, and I trip over you two making out under a bush." She looked pointedly at Lucie. "What a floozy."

Steffi didn't wait for a response, didn't check the sight-lines from here to the bench, just went marching down the path with a big show of indignation and disgust.

As soon as she was gone, Lucie unwound herself from Ian, but she pulled the camera out from behind her back. Standing in the middle of the path, she said tightly, "Yeah, well, Steffi, here's a news flash. I may be a floozy, but at least I have the class to do it with the right man."

There was a long pause. The night was still and humid, and the mourning dove hooted again, long and plaintive.

"What did you mean by that?" Ian asked quietly.

"What?"

"The right man. You said you had the class to do it with the right man." He waited. And she tried to think of a way to explain it away. She didn't suppose "Freudian slip" would get her anywhere.

"Nothing," she said eventually. "I didn't mean anything. Just that I'm with you, the man I'm supposed to be with." Not terribly persuasive. "I mean, the man people expect me to be with, given the fact that they *think* we're together. So if I'm in the bushes with anyone, well, it would naturally be you."

Ian edged around in front of her, forcing her to look at him. *Uh-oh.* In the heavy, warm June air, with only a small sliver of a moon to break the darkness, she felt awfully vulnerable. Besides, he knew how to push all her buttons.

Although at the moment, it looked more like she was pushing his.

"Lucie," he began, in a hushed, tense tone, but broke

off. Clenching his hands into fists, he cursed under his breath, wheeled away, and then turned back. "Listen, I know I'm not your type—you've made that clear—but would you ever think that I *am* the right man? For real? Would you?"

Lucie's head was spinning. "I—I don't know what to say."

Was this a test? She searched his face for clues, but the light was too dim to tell. Did he want her to laugh it off and leap onto him and giggle that he was exactly the right man and she would be happy to prove it back in their room? No, that seemed way too dopey and infantile.

So maybe his pride was hurt because she had so unceremoniously dismissed his hypothetical marriage proposal. *You're very marriable, Ian. I'm sure millions of women would love to catch you, just not me...*

Condescending.

And if she blurted, *I am so head over heels in love with you I can't see straight*, would he shoot out of there like a jack-rabbit?

She wanted to say it, to confess her deepest feelings. But that's just not how she and Ian did things.

"Never mind," he mumbled, backing away. "That's okay. Forget I said anything. I, uh, must've been out of my mind for a minute."

As he strode away in the black night, beating a hasty retreat back to the house, Lucie lingered on the path. Feeling like dirt, she kicked at a small piece of gravel.

"Out of your mind?" she asked no one in particular. "You got that one right, Lucie."

A NEW DAY had dawned in the Mackintosh household. Except this morning, Lucie woke up alone. She thought that was what she wanted. Turned out she was wrong.

"Not the first time for that, is it?" she berated herself. "Face it, Lucie. You blew it."

Lonely, melancholy, miserable, she was swimming in a sea of all the negative emotions she normally refused to feel.

Too bad. She'd had all night to think about it. Examined and re-examined every nook and cranny of her bizarre relationship with Ian. Her conclusion?

"He liked me. I don't think he expected it any more than I did, but he really liked me. Go figure."

She sighed, tossing herself on the sunny yellow window seat. "He was terrific. He faced down my father, he brought me home to meet his wonderful family, he tried to send up a few trial balloons, and I shot him down." Savagely, she declared, "I threw his pride back in his face and now he will probably never speak to me again." She laughed bitterly. "Heck, he's probably already on the phone with Feather McStupid."

But, hey, at least she had the video tape. It lay on the dresser in her room, as big as life, a 500-pound gorilla that she didn't know what to do with.

Well, that wasn't exactly true. She knew. All she had to do was give Ian the tape, let him save his brother, and it would all be over.

As fast as that.

"Lucie," she said out loud, "you are a positive person, not a moper. So let's save Kyle and get the hell out of here."

Rousing herself, she found a pair of shorts and a cheery yellow top almost the same color as the bed linens on that luscious four-poster. Humming to herself, she energetically packed up the rest of her things and dropped the camera into her purse.

Oh, heavens. Why was she singing "Happy Birthday" again? "If I've learned nothing else from this escapade, I know now to stay away from birthday celebrations," she swore.

She took one last look at the pretty lemon-colored room, her eyes skimming past that beautiful bed. She had no excuse for this one. Maybe the first time she was drunk and the second time, in the closet, she was temporarily insane. But in the bed, when he was sweet and tender and everything went achingly slow...

No excuse.

So she picked up her bags, she closed the door, and went to find Ian. In the library, of course.

He was waiting. No newspaper to hide behind, just the damn gorgeous man himself this time.

Without wasting time on preliminaries, Lucie set down her luggage and dangled the video camera from one hand. "Well, here it is. Kyle's ticket to freedom."

"So." He set his jaw. "This is what we've been waiting for."

"Are you going to show the tape to Kyle or Steffi?"

"Neither." He stood, walking past her, neatly stripping the camera out of her hand without so much as touching her. With a flat smile, he popped the cassette out of the side. "I think I'll just take it straight to your dad. Kill two birds with one stone. He hands over Pandora's Boxers and talks Steffi into a quick, cheap divorce or I put the video on the Internet. That ought to do it. Game, set and match. We win."

Lucie blinked. "But Ian..." This wasn't what she wanted. Getting back Pandora's Boxers fair and square, sure. Saving Kyle from Steffi's evil clutches, sure. But blackmail? Showing her father a video of his beloved princess schtupping a busboy? "Ian, I don't think that's the way to go. It's just so ugly."

He shrugged. "It's ugly however it works."

"Not if you tell Kyle what's on the video and let him talk to Steffi himself," she argued. "I'm sure she'll see reason and my dad would never even have to know."

"In the first place, I don't think she'll see reason. And in the second..." Sending her a level stare, Ian slid his hands into his pockets. When did he get so cold and ruthless? She'd never seen him like this. "Lucie, you're packed and ready to go. So we don't have the couple card to play anymore. Without extra leverage, your father is going to hang on to Pandora's Boxers and your dream is going to shrivel up and die. Do you want to back off and let him win?"

"I don't really care," she insisted. "Making my father miserable has never been high on my agenda."

"I thought you wanted to win."

"No, I wanted my mother's company back." She frowned. "If my dad sees that tape, he's going to be devastated. You know, Steffi always accuses me of trying to ruin her life. And that would be exactly what I'd be doing. Just for spite."

Ian shook his head, implacable. "The deal was that

you helped me get rid of Steffi and I helped you get Pandora's Boxers. One for one. That was the deal. I'm not letting this go only half-finished."

"But I don't want it this way." She tried to reason with him, but it didn't seem to be having any impact at all. "Listen, Ian, when Kyle gets his casts off, he can confront Steffi and ask her for a divorce like thousands of men ask thousands of women for divorces every day. They can handle this. It's not our place to mix it all together with my company into this big, nasty black-mail stew—"

"Lucie," he shot back, "this is what we wanted. This is what we planned. Trust me. It's the right thing to do—for Kyle *and* you."

"It's not what I planned."

But he kept going. He paced nearer, he took her shoulders in his strong hands, and he spoke softly, urgently, as if she were very dim-witted. Or maybe as if she were his wife. Lucie felt a chill seep into her bones. "I know you're angry with me," he said. "You think I pushed you into a sexual relationship that you didn't want. Well, you were there, too, Lucie. You know as well as I do that it was amazing between us. And if that's all it was—a fling—well, so what? Time to get over it and move on."

"I can't believe you're saying this," she whispered.

"But what we did or didn't have together has nothing to do with how the saga of the dirty video plays out," he insisted. "This is what we both knew would happen if we filmed Steffi and Paolo in the act. You're just chickening out at the last minute. It's like a habit.

You've let your father and stepmother and bratty sister treat you like a doormat for so long, you don't know any other way to behave."

"Thank you for painting such a flattering portrait." Lucie licked her lips. "So, doormat that I am, I don't even get to decide what's right for me, apparently."

"Not if you're going to be ridiculous about it," he growled.

"You sound exactly like my father."

He exhaled abruptly. And he said again, "You have to trust me on this."

"Why should I? I don't even know you."

He didn't offer a word in his own defense. She tried to tell herself that this wasn't the real Ian, that he was in a truly awful mood and he would regain his sanity in a few hours or a few days. But what was she supposed to do in the meantime?

If he walked out and rescued his brother and resurrected her company, it really would be all over. Done. Finished. Complete. Up in her room, that had sounded like a sane and rational way to go. Down here, looking at him, with his familiar, clever, sinful hands on her, the idea sent her into a tizzy. She wanted to weep and tell him that he was who she wanted to take her to Paris and forget about boxers or babies or that damned Steffi. *I just want you. I don't want to be done!*

But apparently that was exactly what he wanted.

"Ian, if you do this," she said softly, "that's the end. You and me, this thing we've had together, whatever it is or could be... It could never amount to anything if you don't respect me and my decisions about myself."

"I do respect you," he returned.

"No, you don't." She made one more attempt. "Please don't treat me like what I want, what's right for me, doesn't matter."

"I promised you that I would get Pandora's Boxers back for you." With the cassette clasped firmly in his hand, he backed away. "I can't give you anything else. But I can give you your company." He smiled, with a spark of the Ian she knew, the one she'd fallen in love with. "It's the least I can do."

"Ian..."

But he was gone.

LUCIE'S FATHER SAT behind a huge, polished desk, in an immense leather chair that looked more like a throne.

"Please, Ian, have a seat," he said jovially, indicating a smaller, much less imposing chair.

"I'd rather stand." Tense, impatient, Ian prepared to get right to the point. He wanted this over with, to put Pandora's Boxers into Lucie's hands, to prove once and for all that it could be handled his way—no muss, no fuss—no matter what she thought. So he said, "Here's the deal, Don. You're going to give Lucie her mother's company. Lock, stock and barrel. We can make it hard, or we can make it easy. But the end result will be the same."

"Now just a minute, young man," Mr. Webster huffed. "I'm making allowances for the fact that you're young and in love with my daughter, but that goes only so far."

Ian waved away his objections. "You and I both

know you're not exactly standing on the moral high ground. You should've given it to her years ago."

The older man chuckled. "Turns out that silly little brassiere and panty factory turns a tidy profit. Who'd have guessed? Just between you and me, Lucie is a sweet girl, but she isn't capable of the hard decisions it takes to run a business." He shook his head sadly. "When push comes to shove, Lucie will fold every time rather than hurt someone's feelings. Feelings! As if that matters in business."

Ian really wished the old man would shut up. His blunt, unkind remarks sounded an awful lot like what Ian had said to Lucie herself. And he didn't like the reminder. Or the comparison.

Donald Webster lit up a fat cigar, blowing malodorous smoke out over the desk. "So why should I turn over a profitable enterprise to my flighty, irresponsible daughter? What's in it for me?"

"Besides the knowledge that you did the honorable thing, you mean?" Ian leaned in over the desk, not flinching when smoke blew in his face. "Why should you give Lucie the company she wants? Because you're right—I am in love with your daughter and that changes everything."

I am in love with your daughter and that changes everything. Where had those words come from?

He hadn't planned to say that. He hadn't been aware he felt it. But once the confession left his lips, it was as if a long, dark hood had been ripped off his head.

Good God! He was in love with her. How could he not know that? But when did it happen?

In love. The forever kind. With Lucie, of all people. Lucie and her impractical underwear. Lucie and her creative ways to make love. Lucie and her wild, sensational, red-gold hair. Lucie and her pale skin that always seemed to be blushing into a rosy glow. Lucie and her laughter and her smile and her complicated, nonlinear, out-of-nowhere ideas.

"I don't see how what you feel for Lucie makes a rat's rear end of difference," her father announced sourly.

"I've been an idiot," Ian said slowly. "A total and complete idiot. But no more. I *am* in love with your daughter."

"Yes, yes, I've got that. So what?"

Ian narrowed his eyes. Back to business. He could puzzle through the repercussions of his love life on his own time. But this, this was for Lucie. "The fact that I care about Lucie means that I'm not going to stand around and let you yank her chain. I don't really care how you feel about Pandora's Boxers. Lucie loves that company. Lucie wants it. Lucie gets it."

Don smiled, chomping down on his stogie. "Since we last spoke, I've done a little checking on you, Ian. I know you have a sizable bankroll, so it's certainly possible that we might do business. It's possible I might be persuaded to let you acquire a certain interest in the enterprise we've been discussing."

"An interest? I don't think so. Not good enough."

"I don't know. I don't think I can just kiss the whole thing goodbye." Stubborn to the last, her father maintained, "I'm fond of that company."

"You did your checking. You know about my bank-roll." Ian's gaze was steady. "Do you really want to fight me on this?" He played his best card, or at least the best one he was willing to toss down at this juncture. He was determined to pluck Pandora's Boxers out of the old man's grasp without bringing up Steffi, unless he absolutely had to. "Do you really want me to launch a big, ugly legal battle? Poor Lucie, wrongfully deprived of her mother's legacy all those years ago. I've got the time, I've got the money, I've got the lawyers, I've got the motivation. And you will lose more than just your boxers."

"Lawyers?"

He bit. He bit! The hook was in Don Webster's mouth and all he had to do was reel him in. "I'm prepared to fight a PR battle as well as a legal one," Ian continued. "Your name will be mud. Let's see, you have a catering company, a chain of dry cleaners, and a few other small holdings, all with your muddy name on them. Compared to losing the whole enchilada, you can afford to part with one small bra-and-panty company, can't you?"

Webster smashed the rest of his cigar into an ashtray. "Perhaps I could see my way clear to letting Lucie have the company she wants. My objection was purely because I was afraid she couldn't handle it. But as long as she has the good sense to stick with you..." The old man smiled weakly. "Well, I know you'll keep her out of trouble."

"Keep Lucie out of trouble?" Ian laughed out loud. "You really don't know her very well, do you?"

"Well, I…"

"Never mind." He waved a hand at Don Webster. "Here's what you're going to do. You're going to get together the paperwork and wrap it up with a big bow."

A bow… Ian was suddenly seized with a brilliant idea. Fragments, possibilities, spun through his brain.

Lucie was furious with him. She also thought he was the wrong man for her. Yet he had just discovered he loved her. So how could he prove to her that he was the right man, and that he belonged back in her life? He'd been holding on to some vague notion that he could offer Pandora's Boxers up like a gift, to prove his sincerity.

But what if he went further than just a gift? What if he upped the ante and turned it into a major production?

"Wrap it up like a present," he said quickly. "A birthday present. And you'll need to bring it, in person, to a party I'm arranging next Saturday night. You see, Lucie turned thirty *last* Saturday night, and I don't think that milestone got the attention it deserved."

"Perhaps—"

"Don't mess with me. I am a desperate man," he interrupted, as his idea began to take shape. "No *perhaps*. This is going to happen."

He barely registered Donald Webster's slow nod.

"Don't disappoint me, Don. Next Saturday. Come with Pandora's Boxers in hand."

Starting to whistle "Happy Birthday," Ian slapped

the desk and made for the door. But on his way over the threshold, he stopped.

"I almost forgot." He turned back, sliding the videocassette out from his inside jacket pocket. "I think you should know that your other daughter is cheating on my brother with a busboy. I haven't said anything to Kyle yet. But you might want to convince her to file a quick annulment and get out of town for a few days. I hear she's hot to go to Hawaii."

"What?" Now he was on his feet. "What kind of joke...?"

"It's not a joke." Ian set the tape on the desk. "The Hawaii thing is just a thought. It's up to you. Although I'd suggest you probably don't want to look at the video. Lucie seems to think it will upset you."

As he cleared the outside of the building, Ian turned his face into the bright summer sun and took a deep breath.

He'd won this round, no matter how Don Webster handled the Steffi situation. But now Ian had better things to think about, like what kind of party to throw for Lucie...and how to get her to show up.

He muttered, "It isn't going to be easy."

10

LUCIE SAT on the floor of her cottage, folding lingerie and briefs to pack away, and perusing the real estate listings from a nearby newspaper at the same time.

"Maybe I should buy a condo," she pondered. "That might be fun."

She hadn't seen her dad, his wife, or their daughter since she'd been back from the Mackintosh mansion. But every time she angled her car past their squatty brown house, she felt major guilt. She debated going in and seeing if they were all right after Ian's big video showdown, if that was indeed what had transpired, but she just couldn't make herself do it.

She didn't want to get yelled at. She didn't even want to know what happened.

Call her a chicken—and Ian had—but that was the way it was. How strange to realize that after all these years, she didn't much care whether her father approved or disapproved of anything she did, that there was no reason to wait for him to turn over Pandora's Boxers. Why bother? So she wouldn't get the name or the assets. So she would be starting from scratch. She'd prefer her mother's name on the company, of course, but it didn't have to be there. She would know in her heart how much a part of it her mother was.

"Maybe I will call it Pandora's Daughter. Or go a whole different direction and make it Lucie's Lingerie. Lucie's Loungewear. Lucie's lascivious, lovely, lacy, little... Hmm."

Oh well. She had plenty of time to think about that.

She tossed another pile of samples into a wardrobe box. Whatever she decided to do about her lingerie business, she didn't want to do it here. Not with that big brown house looming nearby like a poisonous mushroom.

Her feelings indicated to her that it was time to move. She'd lived in the little cottage ever since her mother died, so it was well past time that she put it behind her and struck out on her own. She had a job and she'd been paying rent for the cottage since she was eighteen, so she could certainly afford an apartment or a house like anyone else.

As she frowned at the listings, wondering where she most wanted to go, her doorbell rang. "Who can that be?" she asked out loud. She felt a small flutter of apprehension in case it was her father or—God forbid— Ian. But either of those seemed unlikely.

If they'd wanted to talk to her, they'd had days. With nary a peep from either of them, the odds seemed good that they weren't interested in making contact.

So Lucie steeled herself, put on a smile, and pulled open the door.

"Lucie Webster?" the delivery man asked, holding out a clipboard.

"Yes." Her interest piqued, she signed her name and took the bulky package. She didn't recognize the return address, although it said it was from something called Festivité. It sounded artsy, but she wasn't expecting any fabric or patterns. It was the right size for something like a basketball, but it seemed awfully light.

Shaking it, Lucie shut the door and brought the mysterious box into her breakfast nook. Setting it down on the table, she went after the scissors, which took a few minutes, since they weren't where they were supposed to be.

And then, scissors in hand, she contemplated the package. Who the heck was Festivité? Or was that just a cover for a letter bomb from Steffi? Or maybe an eviction notice and accompanying materials from her father?

"Better to find out than stand here and worry about it," she decided. She attacked it with her shears, slashing at the thick tape, wrenching open cardboard flaps, revealing...

A balloon. A shiny silver Mylar balloon filled with helium.

There was a big star on it, and it read, "You're invited!" It floated lazily out of the box, scattering bright, metallic confetti shaped like stars, and trailing a thick, square white card tied to the curling ribbons.

Her name, inscribed in hot pink ink, spiraled across the front of the envelope. How very entertaining. She didn't know anyone who went to this much trouble to create cool invitations, but hey, maybe someone was having a particularly inspired baby shower or pool party.

Lucie detached the envelope from the balloon and quickly tore it open. "Huh. 'You are cordially invited...'" She skimmed to the bottom. "It's from Ian's parents."

This was odd. Incredible, unexpected and downright odd. After disappearing from their house like a thief in the night, leaving no traces except for one vandalized linen closet and one enraged son, she didn't expect to hear from them again, and especially not to get invited to any parties they were hosting. Of course, she had told Jessica she would make her some yoga clothes, but this didn't look like it had anything to do with yoga.

She scanned the lines. "'You are cordially invited to a soiree in honor of a special birthday. Please help us celebrate the thirtieth anniversary of the birth of our dear friend Lucie...' Oh, my God."

The invitation wobbled in her hand.

"The party is for me."

But how could that be? She read it again. *In honor of a special birthday... Our dear friend Lucie Webster...*

Yes, it was definitely for her. Her heart warmed and swelled in her chest. What a sweet gesture from the Mackintosh clan.

But why? How did they even know it was her birthday? And why did they care?

"Well, his mother did like me," she mused. "And I liked her, too. Maybe I mentioned I'd just had my birthday."

But that was still no reason for Myra and George

Mackintosh to throw her a party. No, she was stumped. This was really out of nowhere.

"Okay, now what?" she asked herself. "Do I go? How can I not go if the party's for me? But how can I go, considering the way Ian and I left things, and if I see him again, I have no idea how I'll react or he'll react or whether he'll even want to see me or I'll want to see him?"

She paced back and forth, chewing on the edge of the invitation. "This could be some matchmaking scheme of his mother's, in which case Ian would hate it—and hate me for going along with it. Or it could be exactly what it says it is—just a party, like a consolation prize for losing Ian, because his mom feels sorry for me now that I'm just flotsam and jetsam left in his wake. And I swear..." Her voice grew louder, more adamant and she began to smack the card against the edge of the table. Thwack. Thwack. Thwack. "If he's there with a date, like that horrid Feather, I really will kill him. No mercy."

Abandoning the battered invitation, she crossed her arms over her chest. "That would be just like him, to bring Feather and flaunt her in my face. As if to say, see, Lucie, what you could've had, and now I am *so* out of your reach. And I wouldn't have a choice—I would have to kill him."

No jury in the world would convict her if they got a glimpse of Feather.

"But if he brings a date, does that mean I should bring a date?" She ran a hand over her forehead. "And if so, who? No. No, wait. This is getting way too complicated. No, no matter what he does, I am not bringing a date. If it's wrong for him, it's wrong for me, and I am not going to stoop to that level just because I think he might."

Lucie paused, losing some of her indignation. "So," she murmured, "I guess that means I'm going."

She had to find out what it was all about, didn't she? She couldn't just leave it a mystery. Besides, she needed to bring those yoga clothes to Jessica and apologize to Myra for vanishing so abruptly.

"Okay. Good." With that settled, she whipped the card back in front of her eyes. "Saturday, eight o'clock. The Highland Inn. No RSVP necessary."

The Highland Inn... She dropped into a kitchen chair. They really were bringing this thing full circle, weren't they?

LUCIE HUDDLED behind the wheel of her newly repaired Jeep, trying to be inconspicuous, watching seconds tick off on her watch. This time, she'd been sure not to park under any balconies, but she peered up there anyway, looking out for airborne missiles from unhappy brides. As she peeked out under the sun visor, she wondered why there were so many cars in the parking lot, too many for one little birthday party.

"They're probably golfing," she said out loud. "I'll bet like three total are here for the party."

Ian's car was conspicuously absent, as was Steffi's little red convertible.

"Whew. That's a relief," she told herself with spirit. "Probably neither one of them will be here."

The clock on the dashboard said 8:11. But her watch was back at 8:04. Was that late enough to go in? How terrible to be the first guest at a party given in your honor. Or the last.

"What if I'm the only guest who shows?" she thought, seized with fresh panic.

Oh, jeez. This was worse than being the hostess.

"Okay, Lucie, you're going in." She took a deep breath, reached over for the purse she'd made up to match her slinky dress, and hopped out of the Jeep. She'd used a basic pattern for a camisole and slip, but found a beautiful bolt of deep-rose silk, and then added fabric roses in various shades of pink to decorate the evening bag.

It was different from most of her designs, especially since she'd spent so much time on the men's line lately, but she thought it looked really pretty. And if she had to face Ian—maybe Ian with a date—she needed to look good.

Calmly, only a little breathless, she walked around to the front door. The last time she'd seen that door, she was wearing Ian's formal shirt and not much else. Ah, yes. Two weeks ago tomorrow and it felt like 150 years.

A doorman—not wearing a kilt, thank you, but a pair of khaki pants and a polo shirt—opened the heavy door for her, and she had no choice but to waltz right in.

"If you're here for the party, miss, it's in the ballroom," he said. "Do you know where that is?"

"Oh, yes. I've been here before."

But tonight there was no overpowering display of

plaid, no bagpipers, no flickering candles, no threat of the Loch Ness monster rising from the punch bowl. Just balloons and bowls of daisies.

And a ballroom full of people.

She hesitated there, in the doorway to the ballroom. But Mrs. Mackintosh spotted her and came swooping down to greet her.

"Happy birthday, Lucie!" she declared. "Come right in, dear. I'm so happy you made it. It just wouldn't have felt right to celebrate your birthday without you."

"I—I suppose not." She smiled as Mr. Mackintosh and Jessica sped over to hug her and kiss her on the cheek. "This is just beautiful," she said, gazing around, and she meant it. There were balloons everywhere, and streamers and paper lanterns, creating a sort of glowing blur of color. "I can't quite believe this is all for me. Is it someone else's birthday, too?"

"No, dear," Myra laughed. She pressed a cup of punch into Lucie's hand. "You enjoy yourself now. I'll be right back. I have to handle something or other to do with... Well, a surprise," she said with a wave of one hand.

Lucie scanned the ballroom. There were people everywhere, way more people than she thought she knew. But someone had clearly gone through her entire Rolodex. They were all wearing silly party hats and carrying bright paper horns, but she recognized teacher friends, the cast of last year's school play, her book group from the library, her yoga class, even Toby and T-Bone and some other huge guys who must have been the rest of their football team.

It seemed as if everyone she'd ever met had come to this crazy birthday party. Everyone except Ian. Or maybe he was hiding in a corner somewhere, making out with Feather.

Lucie shook it off. It was a lovely party, and Mrs. Mackintosh deserved better than a morose guest of honor.

"Hmm... I don't think I've ever been a guest of honor before," she murmured as she sipped her punch.

"Happy birthday, Ms. Webster!" A former student hovered at her elbow, dying to talk about what she'd been doing since she graduated, and Lucie gladly took the distraction. She was enjoying the tail end of a story about dormitory life at college when they were joined by, of all people, Baker Burns. Finishing her tale, her former student excused herself to get a cup of punch.

"Oh, Baker," she said immediately, "I'm so sorry. I never heard what happened to you that night. Is it only two weeks ago? Steffi's wedding, I mean."

"Oh, that." He shrugged. "I'll tell you the whole story sometime, but it really turned out, well, bizarre. Good bizarre," he added quickly. "But bizarre. I was already asleep, and this woman came bursting into my hotel room. This gorgeous woman. I still don't know why she picked my room or how she got in there—she's not clear on that herself—but she needed first aid and, well, some TLC." He grinned. "Turns out we really hit it off, and we've been together ever since."

"No..." Lucie's jaw dropped. "Don't tell me...?"

"Uh-huh. Her name is Feather," he said happily.

"She's a little younger than I am, so I'm taking it slow, but I really think this could be something."

"How nice for you," she managed. "Is she...?"

"Here? Tonight? Yes, she is." He glanced around. "She didn't remember your name from the wedding, but, of course, this place is special to us, so she wanted to come to the party. I think she slipped off to the ladies' room. I'll try to catch you later to introduce you."

"She's in the ladies' room? And she doesn't know me by name? Oh, you know what, you don't need to track the poor thing down just to introduce her to me. I'm sure you're..." Lucie wracked her brain. "I'm sure you have better things to do, you two young lovers, you. I'm just really pleased that you came tonight, Baker, and that you are so happy with, um, Feather. You just never know what fate has in store for you, do you?"

"You can say that again." With the same dazed look of bliss radiating from his face, Baker disappeared into the crowd.

"It's time, Lucie!" Jessica cried. "Ta-da!"

"Time for what?"

But as she watched, wide-eyed, a man wheeled in a table overflowing with gaily wrapped presents. And right behind him, another waiter steered a cart carrying a huge, blazing birthday cake.

"I've never seen anything like that in my life," she murmured. Was someone going to jump out of that thing? Ian, in black velvet briefs with a silver star over the fly?

But no. Nothing like that. Sometimes a cake was just a cake.

Everybody was singing "Happy Birthday" at the top of their lungs, urging her to step up and blow out the candles, so she did. She laughed. It was a beautiful cake and a beautiful moment, and she realized somehow, through all the haze from the candles and the good wishes, that she really was thirty years old. Thirty. *My, my*.

"I'm thirty, I've never been to Paris, and I'm alone at my birthday party," she said to no one in particular. "And I don't know what's wrong with me, dwelling on these gloomy thoughts. Shame on me."

"Shame on you? There's no shame on you today, young lady." George Mackintosh pressed a plate of birthday cake and a fork into her hand. "It's your birthday!"

"It's really not," she tried to tell him. "It was really two weeks ago."

"Lucie, try the cake. You have to have the first slice."

"Oh, okay." Carrot cake. Her favorite. Who in the world knew that? "It's delicious."

"Good." Ian's father waited patiently until she was done with her cake, and then he took the plate, caught her hand, and dragged her over to the gift table. "Don't mean to rush you, but we're on a timetable here."

"We are?" But there was no opportunity to question him about the schedule. "Good heavens. I can't imagine where all these gifts came from."

"The people who love you," he said kindly, pulling a chair up for her.

Speaking of love, where the hell is your son? she wanted to shout. *Where the hell is Ian?*

She refrained. It was hard to yell at people when they were being so incredibly generous and nice. Jessica popped up to hand over gifts, apparently quite concerned that they be opened in a specific order, and Lucie obliged, oohing and aahing appropriately over the antique teapot from his parents, the M&M dispenser, the "Flirty at Thirty" T-shirt, and even the waffle iron.

That made her scan the ballroom for Steffi, but she didn't see any signs of her.

Kyle, however, did make an appearance, hobbling up on his crutches to drop a gift bag into her lap. "I wasn't late," he asserted. "I was just sitting over on the edge with my legs propped up. But I wasn't late. I swear I wasn't late."

"Kyle, it's okay." She smiled, wondering what all the fuss was about. "I don't care if you were late. I mean, good heavens, you have two broken legs. It's a miracle you're here at all. Not to mention the fact that you brought me a gift." She put aside the tissue paper and lifted out a pair of lavish lace handkerchiefs, just the kind of thing she liked to make sachets or trim camisoles with. "Thank you so much. These are fabulous. So, please, stop worrying."

"Well, I owe you a lot, after all, and Ian told me he'd break both my arms, too, if I was late, and..." He trailed off awkwardly as his little sister tried to elbow him without knocking him off his crutches.

"Ian did *what?* And what do you owe me?" she inquired, totally confused.

"Forget Ian. I wasn't supposed to mention him." He looked sheepish. "But as for the other, it's obvious. I owe you a lot for working so hard to get rid of Steffi. I mean, it was my own fault and I did deserve what I got and it really wasn't your problem. So what you and Ian did... Sorry. Not supposed to mention him. But, anyway, what you did was really great."

Lucie considered her words carefully. Nobody was supposed to mention him... But where was he? Instead, she asked, "And what *did* happen with Steffi?"

"Oh. I guess you haven't heard. Your dad fired the busboy, but sent both of them to the Dominican Republic for Steffi to arrange a quickie divorce." He grinned. "And I am out of the marriage without a whimper. Ian and I... Sorry. I, uh, *we* got our money, too. The sale of m-tosh.com went through a few days ago. So I'm doing great. And I'm never getting married again." He raised a hand off the crossbar of his crutch. "I swear."

"Oh. I see." She still hadn't quite taken in the part about Steffi and the Dominican Republic, let alone the big-money sale Ian had been waiting for. "Terrific. It sounds as if things are going terrific."

"Okay, enough with Kyle. Open my present now," Jessica interrupted, handing over a big box with an enormous bow.

Lucie was so overwhelmed with the crazy atmosphere of this party that she felt like she was operating on automatic pilot. Still, even if Ian never showed up, it seemed clear his family members were not going to let her leave unless she played by their rules and opened every last package. So she unwrapped Jessica's gift neatly and pulled off the lid. "Oh, wow. A new yoga mat and blocks and even a strap. Thank you, Jess. I love it."

She really did love it. And the handkerchiefs and the teapot and even the waffle iron. But finally, thankfully, the stack of presents began to thin out. She was on gift overload by now, not sure who'd given what or whether all this stuff would even fit in her Jeep. Now she understood the proverb about too much of a good thing, especially when she couldn't really enjoy the party, not while she worried that Ian was lurking by a pillar or behind a door.

Face it. He isn't waiting to jump out and surprise you. He isn't coming.

"Oh, look, just one more package," she said brightly, pointing to a small, flat gift left on the table. "Hand me that one, will you, Jess?"

Jessica glanced at her watch. "We're a little early for that one." She hesitated. "Do you want some more cake?"

"No, not really." She chewed her lip, peering at the mysterious last gift more closely. *Don't get too excited,* she commanded herself. *It's not the right shape for a ring. And it's not some sweepingly romantic gesture from Ian because Ian isn't here and, besides, he would never give you a ring this way because he knows you wouldn't take it.*

Maybe a bracelet? What would Ian think up if he were thinking up sweepingly romantic gestures?

"Probably underwear," she said under her breath. Something skimpy and sexy, something with bells and leather and corset strings, something only a guy would appreciate. Her mind was whirling. And he'd want her to model it for him, and even though it fit like a vise, they both knew she'd do it because she hadn't seen him in eight days and about now she would do whatever he wanted. "Are you sure I can't open that now?" she ventured. "What could it hurt—?"

"Nope." Jessica folded her arms, flicking her eyes down to her wristwatch again. "Not yet."

"Wait, wait, here's another present!" a gruff voice said heartily.

"Dad?" She looked up. Yep, that's who it was. Running in from the doorway, he was hauling a box even bigger than the one with all the yoga equipment, wrapped in garish birthday paper, garnished with a floppy orange bow the size of his head. "I'm really surprised to see you. What are you doing here?"

"Sorry I'm late. Your boyfriend threatened me with all kinds of things if I was late and I tried my best." He extended the gigantic box. "But here we go. I made it."

"Apparently there's some sort of timetable I'm not aware of," Lucie noted dryly. Focusing on Jessica, she asked, "Is it okay to open this one?"

"Uh-huh. Actually, you were supposed to do his present first, but he's late." She arched an eyebrow— shades of her imperious older brother—and glared at Don Webster. "He is very late."

"Then I guess we'd better take care of it ASAP." The sooner she got through this one, the sooner she got back to the puzzle in the flat package that she was almost certain was from Ian. So she ripped off the paper and ribbon carelessly and tossed them aside. "What is it, Dad? A beachball?" she joked.

But all it seemed to be was tissue paper.

She kept poking further and further into the box, until she retrieved a thick envelope taped to the bottom. "Well, let me guess." But she already knew before she opened it or looked at the documents inside. "Did Ian... Did he arrange this?"

"He had something to do with it." Her dad backed up. "But it's yours now. All of it. It was your mother's and it's what she would've wanted and I'm sorry, Lucie. Anyway, it's yours now."

It was the closest to an apology—or even an understanding—she had ever gotten from her father. "Thank you," she said simply. "I think you know how much this means to me."

"Happy birthday, dear. And now..." He backed away nervously. "I have to be going. But happy birthday."

"Thanks." She smiled. "It really is. You never get everything you want, but you know, this birthday, I came about as close as humanly possible. Don't you think, Jess?"

"Um, you have another present to open, Lucie." Her blue eyes were the same shade as Ian's when she held out the last gift. "Ready?"

"Ready if you are." Not undies. Not from Ian. She realized that now. He wouldn't direct his innocent teenage sister to hand over a box of slutty lingerie. So...what?

Her hand trembled as she pulled off the ribbon. It wasn't even wrapped, just a plain white box. When she lifted the lid, she was still bewildered. She picked it up, dangling it by the red cord. "But this looks like..."

It was a small plaid bag, just big enough to hold, oh, maybe a few condoms and a tube of Poisonberry Smog lipstick.

"What is it, Lucie?" Jessica asked with excitement. "What did he give you?"

"You remember, Jess. It's the purse the bridesmaids carried at Kyle's wedding." She shrugged. "That was the night we, uh, met, so I guess he's reminding me—"

"But what's inside?"

"Oh. Inside. I didn't think..." Carefully, not anxious to spill a pile of condoms in her lap in front of a minor, Lucie separated the fabric folds and peeked inside. "It's..." Something shiny. She fished it out and held it up. "A key."

She already knew and she was already on her feet. Of course she should've trusted him to know exactly the right sweepingly romantic gesture. She breathed a sigh of relief and joy. "It's the key to room 203."

Euphoria and anticipation splashed through her veins, pushing her out of the ballroom, but she turned back. "Jess, thank you so much and please tell your parents thank you, too. I love all of you."

"Go!" Jessica yelled impatiently. "He's waiting for you."

She went. Lucie's feet felt light enough to fly up the

stairs, but her hand was shaking so hard she could barely get the key in the lock. "Oh, sure, *now* you fumble. When it counted, you worked like a locksmith."

But finally, the key turned, the knob rotated under her fingers, and the door slid open. She was having trouble breathing and her heart was in her throat, but otherwise, she was feeling just fine.

Lucie stepped over the threshold.

She saw an array of candlesticks, maybe six or seven, giving the room a flickering glow. She saw the big four-poster with its heavy drapes, a silver bucket holding a bottle of champagne on ice, and a crystal bowl brimming over with familiar packets, the condom kind. There was even another birthday gift—just when she was thoroughly sick of birthday gifts—wrapped and set next to the bowl.

But no Ian.

Maybe he was in the bed behind those curtains. Maybe he wanted to reenact the whole thing and she was supposed to strip and jump in there with him. Yes? Or no? If she peeled off her clothes, would she feel stupid when he came bounding into the room with a bagpipe band to recreate the Scottish mood of their first night together?

Just when she was about to swoon with frustration and indecision, telling herself she could not take one more second of this Invisible Man routine, he stepped out from behind the bed, his hand on the footpost.

She'd never seen him in a tuxedo. Stunning. Sweepingly romantic. "Wow. Black tie. And here I thought I might find you naked in the bed, waiting for me."

"Looking forward to that?"

Mischievous, she whispered, "Maybe."

But a pause hung between them. Ian crossed to her. Not touching her—purposely, she sensed—he asked softly, "So, am I forgiven? I took the tape to your father, Lucie. I didn't blackmail him, though. Well, not the way you meant—"

"Ian, it's okay. I just saw him and he doesn't seem to be any the worse for wear. And we both got what we wanted. Pandora's Boxers. Kyle's freedom." She smiled, restless, anxious. "You know me—I don't hold a grudge. Doormats don't hold grudges."

"Lucie, you are not a doormat and I am so sorry I ever said that." His eyes were imploring. "I got all mixed up with pride and stupidity. I wanted to give you something."

"Quit beating yourself up." She lifted her shoulders in a small shrug. *Touch me. Take me.* "I'm not mad. Do I look mad?"

"You look incredible." The light in his eyes had shifted. No more apologies. Now his gaze held heat and a potent flame of desire. That was more like it. He reached out one finger to touch a tendril of her hair, to follow its path down her neck and around the slippery, fragile strap of her camisole.

"I missed you," she said simply.

A crooked smile curved his lips. "God, I missed you. You just don't turn a man on like that and then walk out, you know?"

"I know how you feel." Brother, did she.

"But I have to tell you the truth. I love you," he said darkly. "I want forever with you."

"You don't have to promise that. I know how you feel about long-term relationships," she tried, sliding her hand over his cheek and his hard jawline. "You were very up-front about that."

Couldn't he see that she just wanted to go to bed with him, to make love about twenty times really fast or really slow or whatever he wanted? Couldn't they do that and *then* talk about forever?

But Ian didn't give up. "Lucie, I know I'm not exactly husband material. *You* were very up-front about that. But the weird thing is, I think we could do really well together. Jeez, listen to me—now Kyle's telling *me* marriage is for idiots and I'm the one telling him it could be fabulous if you just find the right woman."

"Um, Ian," she interjected, hoping to get a word in. "Are you asking me to marry you?"

He got very wary all of a sudden. "No, not if you don't want me to." He paused. "Do you want me to?"

"If you want to."

"Of course I do."

"You do?"

"Yes," he said eagerly. "I know you want to go to Paris and that's fine. That's great. The tickets are in the box on the desk. That's your real birthday present."

"What? No!" Lucie sent a quick glance over to the package. "Paris?" she squealed, throwing her arms around his neck. "Really? And we can walk in the rain and will you read me sonnets? I am *so* going to marry you!"

His eyes searched hers. Softly, he asked, "You're serious? You're really saying yes?"

"Of course I'm saying yes." She loved him so much she could feel it every time she breathed. "After you got back Pandora's Boxers for me, and this wonderful birthday party, how could I not marry you? Ian, I loved you the first time I saw you in your kilt at the altar. I lied. You are *so* my type." She couldn't keep the little quaver out of her voice. "I just didn't think I was yours."

He exhaled deeply, then he held her pressed close in a hard, tight embrace. Into her ear, he whispered, "You're mine."

Lucie framed his gorgeous face with her hands, looked at him for a long moment, and then kissed him sweet and long. "This is the most incredible way to celebrate your birthday, I have to tell you."

He grinned, swinging her up into his arms and moving for the bed. "Just wait till you see what I do next year." He nibbled her ear and slipped the strap off one shoulder. "You like surprises, don't you?"

Lucie laughed. "I do now."

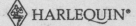

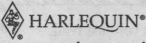

You're not going to believe this offer!

In October and November 2000, buy any two Harlequin or Silhouette books and save $10.00 off future purchases, or buy any three and save $20.00 off future purchases!

Just fill out this form and attach 2 proofs of purchase (cash register receipts) from October and November 2000 books and Harlequin will send you a coupon booklet worth a total savings of $10.00 off future purchases of Harlequin and Silhouette books in 2001. Send us 3 proofs of purchase and we will send you a coupon booklet worth a total savings of $20.00 off future purchases.

Saving money has never been this easy.

I accept your offer! Please send me a coupon booklet:

Name: _____

Address: _____ City: _____

State/Prov.: _____ Zip/Postal Code: _____

Optional Survey!

In a typical month, how many Harlequin or Silhouette books would you buy <u>new</u> at retail stores?

☐ Less than 1   ☐ 1   ☐ 2   ☐ 3 to 4   ☐ 5+

Which of the following statements best describes how you <u>buy</u> Harlequin or Silhouette books? Choose one answer only that <u>best</u> describes you.

☐ I am a regular buyer and reader
☐ I am a regular reader but buy only occasionally
☐ I only buy and read for specific times of the year, e.g. vacations
☐ I subscribe through Reader Service but also buy at retail stores
☐ I mainly borrow and buy only occasionally
☐ I am an occasional buyer and reader

Which of the following statements best describes how you <u>choose</u> the Harlequin and Silhouette series books you buy <u>new</u> at retail stores? By "series," we mean books within a particular line, such as *Harlequin PRESENTS* or *Silhouette SPECIAL EDITION*. Choose one answer only that <u>best</u> describes you.

☐ I only buy books from my favorite series
☐ I generally buy books from my favorite series but also buy books from other series on occasion
☐ I buy some books from my favorite series but also buy from many other series regularly
☐ I buy all types of books depending on my mood and what I find interesting and have no favorite series

---

Please send this form, along with your cash register receipts as proofs of purchase, to:
In the U.S.: Harlequin Books, P.O. Box 9057, Buffalo, NY 14269
In Canada: Harlequin Books, P.O. Box 622, Fort Erie, Ontario L2A 5X3
(Allow 4-6 weeks for delivery) Offer expires December 31, 2000

PHQ4002

Tyler Brides

It happened one weekend...

Quinn and Molly Spencer are delighted to accept three
bookings for their newly opened B&B, Breakfast Inn Bed,
located in America's favorite hometown, Tyler, Wisconsin.

But Gina Santori is anything but thrilled to discover her
best friend has tricked her into sharing a room with
the man who broke her heart eight years ago....

And Delia Mayhew can hardly believe that she's
gotten herself locked in the Breakfast Inn Bed
basement with the sexiest man in America.

Then there's Rebecca Salter. She's turned up at the
Inn in her wedding gown. Minus her groom.

*Come home to Tyler for three delightful novellas
by three of your favorite authors: Kristine Rolofson,
Heather MacAllister and Jacqueline Diamond.*

HARLEQUIN®
Makes any time special ™

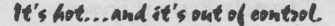

Pamela Burford presents

The Wedding Ring

Four high school friends and a pact—
every girl gets her ideal mate by thirty or be
prepared for matchmaking! The rules are
simple. Give your "chosen" man three
months...and see what happens!

Love's Funny That Way
Temptation #812—on sale December 2000
It's no joke when Raven Muldoon falls in love with comedy
club owner Hunter—*brother* of her "intended."

I Do, But Here's the Catch
Temptation #816—on sale January 2001
Charli Ross is more than willing to give up her status as
last of a dying breed—the thirty-year-old virgin—to Grant.
But all *he* wants is marriage.

One Eager Bride To Go
Temptation #820—on sale February 2001
Sunny Bleecker is still waiting tables at Wafflemania when
Kirk comes home from California and wants to marry her.
It's as if all her dreams have finally come true—except...

Fiancé for Hire
Temptation #824—on sale March 2001
No way is Amanda Coppersmith going to let
The Wedding Ring rope her into marriage. But no matter
how clever she is, Nick is one step ahead of her...

"Pamela Burford creates the
memorable characters readers love!"
—The Literary Times